Grandma
Nuh Easy at All

Josephine Gooden

LMH PUBLISHING LIMITED

Edited by: Tony Patel
Cover Illustration: Courtney Lloyd Robinson
Cover Design: Keneisha Arch
Typeset & book layout: Keneisha Arch

Published by: LMH Publishing Limited
Suite 10-11, Sagicor Industrial Park
7 Norman Road, Kingston C.S.O., Jamaica
Tel.: (876) 938-0005; Fax: (876) 759-8752
Email: lmhbookpublishing@cwjamaica.com
Websites: www.lmhpublishing.com & www.lmhdigital.com

Print in the U.S.A.   ISBN: 978-976-8245-26-7

NATIONAL LIBRARY OF JAMAICA CATALOGUING-IN-PUBLICATION DATA

Gooden, Josephine
    Grandma nuh easy at all / Josephine Gooden

    pages; cm.

ISBN 978-976-8245-26-7 (pbk)

1.   Jamaican fiction
I.   Title

813   dc 23

Contents

CHAPTER
One

It was a beautiful summer morning. Grandma Hazel was usually awakened at 6 a.m. by the crowing of her roosters and the loud blowing of horns from passing market trucks. Since she did not believe in modern technology and refused to accept it even when offered, she relied on nature to tell the time and weather conditions.

Grandma Hazel's first action before she began her day was to kneel down and pray with her family kneeling beside her.

Grandma Hazel prepared 'feed' for the fowls early in the morning so that they could lay eggs, enough to sell at the market close by. She then prepared breakfast, which she called 'wash mouth', being the first meal to go in the mouth.

Grandma Hazel's great grandson Timothy, was spending the summer holidays with her. Grandma Hazel peeked over her huge lenses, which were held together by thick, aged, yellow, plastic frames. She pointed her thick jointed finger, restricted by arthritis and a neglected broken bone. "Bwoy go tek off yuh grampa trouses!" she shouted at Timothy, her face masked in disgust.

"Is not grampa pants Grandma, is mine," Timothy answered.

1

"What mek de waise so big dat yuh haffi hole it up wid yuh han', an' yuh bat bat outa doah?"

"Is the style Grandma, t'ings and time change. You have to get use to the changes," he replied, looking at Grandma Hazel from the corner of his eyes.

"Style!" she shouted, her eyes widening. Her neck stretched like a rooster crowing in anger. "Style mek yuh ah wear trouses dat mek yuh walk like when baby a walk wid dem nappy full a kaka?" Grandma Hazel asked.

"Is modern time now Grandma, you have to get use to it," Timothy replied.

"Get use to yuh madness bwoy? What a way yuh fawud! Move outa mi way bwoy!" she shouted, trying to stand on feet constricted by age. "Where mi put mi spectacle?" she asked, looking around.

"Ha ha haah!" Timothy laughed loudly, holding up his pants with one hand and running sideways from his grandmother. Timothy, still laughing said, "You have it on."

She felt her glasses on her face.

"Move outa mi way!" she shouted, clapping her hands on her thighs and looking at Timothy, her face crowned with grief. "Oonuh new generation wi mek de debble mad, cho!"

"Grandma, do you have any stocking can give me one?" Timothy asked. Grandma Hazel placed her hands on her hips, trying to stand tall, but her poor, old skeleton would not allow her.

"Jehovia God help mi! Bwoy! What yuh want stocking fa, yuh a gal pickney? A Miss Flossy yuh a turn inna? A gwine turn yuh ova to de police," Grandma Hazel said, pointing her finger at Timothy.

"No Grandma, I want the stocking to put over mi hair so dat later when mama come I will look cool. I could neva turn gay Grandma," Timothy said as he walked away.

"Gay! Yuh deaf bwoy? Mi no say gay, I seh 'Miss Flossy'."

"Is the same Grandma, and don't worry think about calling police if you hear about any gay man for it legalize almost everywhere now. Even one of the police up at the Top Road Police Station his name is aam, aam, I can't remember, I will tell you his name as soon as I remember Grandma. In every kind of job you find them, man live with man and woman with woman," Timothy said. Grandma Hazel, shaking her head, asked Timothy if he was still smoking the 'stinking bush'. His talk about being gay and stocking for his head had to be the effect of marijuana.

"Go feed the fowl. Dem hungry an' dem making noise, yuh look like a prekeh!" she said, dismissing him.

Timothy's mother Lorna arrived for a visit. "Good morning Grandma," said Lorna, hugging and kissing her.

"Morning," replied Grandma Hazel, wiping her cheek with her apron. "Mi no want no paint on mi face, mi no know what mek oonuh haffi paint up oonuh kin so!"

"Why are you angry Grandma?" Lorna asked.

"No yuh bwoy deh chat madness at mi ears."

"Don't pay Timothy any mind Grandma," Lorna replied.

"Dis a serious matta!" Grandma Hazel said, hitting her cane on the ground, extending her corded neck, her lips buttoned tight as they quivered with anger. "De bwoy smoke de stinkin' bush an' now 'im deh chat pure madness, 'im soon gone a madhouse, an' once 'im foot touch madhouse, 'im done fah! Poor Deloris dead an' gone, God res' her soul, she hab one son name 'Bredda' an' de same stinkin' bush 'im use to smoke. 'Im dead inna madhouse."

She paused and then continued. "From dem put de stiff jacket pan 'im, an' carry him weh, no body see 'im again till 'im dead. De worse t'ing about de whole situation is dat de only way we know seh 'im dead is because 'im duppy use to raise cane in de district. All dem bwoy who use to walk late at night couldn't do dat no more because 'im even climb up inna tree an' jump on people back, I neva hear or si any ghost so prejumpsous."

"No Grandma, Timothy is not mad," Lorna said.

"'Im no mad?" Grandma Hazel asked bending forward, her eyes dilated. "After 'im deh ya a tell mi say man a married man, an' woman a married woman. De bwoy mad more dan shark!"

"Grandma, let me explain," Lorna said. Taking a seat close to her and placing one hand on her shoulder, Lorna spoke in a compassionate voice. "You would not know Grandma but Timothy is right."

"Like muma, like son!" Grandma Hazel said angrily, while pulling her shoulder away from Lorna's hand and cutting her eyes at her.

CHAPTER
Two

Grandma Hazel got up from her seat in a rage. She grabbed her walking stick and hobbled out of the house as fast as her aching legs could take her. It was a windy day, so she stopped to tie her scarf tighter on her head in the shape of a rooster's tail. She suddenly noticed that she had not changed her polka dot stained apron. Grandma Hazel thought of returning home to change it but changed her mind. She did not want Lorna and Timothy to know that she had left the house.

Looking behind her momentarily, making sure Lorna and Timothy were not following her, Grandma Hazel continued her journey to the Ben Tree Police Station.

It was 1 p.m. and the sun was shining brightly while the trees along the road provided partial shade. Grandma Hazel put all the energy she had into walking up the winding parochial road. She walked until her ancient body produced beads of sweat, which dropped like pearls from her face. Grandma Hazel became tired, so she decided to sit under a 'bassida' tree to rest her legs. The birds were chirping loudly while picking at the buds from the tree.

Lorna and her son Timothy tiptoed out of the house trying not to awaken Grandma Hazel. "Poor Grandma, she took it so hard she went to sleep. We must not wake her up," Lorna said, closing the door quietly.

Lorna and Timothy decided to go to the little shop in the village. This took some time as Lorna made frequent stops to see some of her friends whom she had not seen for a while.

As Grandma Hazel wiped sweat from her face with her apron, her attention was drawn by the noisy strutting sound from the boots of an emaciated old man walking towards her. His bearings badly needed oiling. He was ridiculously bony and his wrinkles were so deeply engraved a large fly could hide in them.

The old man stopped under the tree where Grandma Hazel was sitting. "Howde-do madam," he said, taking his hat off and using it to fan his sweaty face. "My name is Ody." He stretched his hand to shake hers.

"My name is Hazel," Grandma Hazel said, shaking his hand.

"May I help you with something?" Ody asked.

"No t'ank yuh sah," Grandma Hazel answered, smiling. Her dimples were as deep as thimbles but she was still a beautiful lady.

"Not even a glass of water?" Ody asked while yawning, his mouth opened like the neck of an old, empty coin purse. Ody sat on a stone. It seemed as if the stone was causing discomfort to his bony buns. He quickly moved and sat on a tree stump. "Look like you are taking a long walk," he said.

"I am walking from Rosetta," she answered.

"Oh my! You live quite a way from here, my God, you mean you walked all the way here? Amazing!" he said.

"Maybe I will go further up de road," Grandma Hazel said. "But..." She stopped talking as she did not want to expose her business.

"When I was a young man, I worked for the govament as a postman," Ody said. He laughed, looking up into the bassida tree, his teeth sticking out like clam shells. They stood one on each side of his month as if in malice with each other.

He continued, "One day mi bicycle chain drop off an' mi haffi walk an' deliver de letta dem. Mi walk, mi walk, a walk so till when mi reach a mi yard, mi haffi mix up salt fisic in de tub an' soak mi foot. Dem time deh, de only shoes mi have was slippas. De one dem what mek outa Dunlop tire-sampatta."

Grandma Hazel smiled. "My first an' only shoes was a crepe, a black crepe."

"Yes," Ody said, "dem use to call dem 'puss boot', now a days dem ya generation have shoes deh stone dog."

"Eh mi dear sah," Grandma Hazel answered.

Ody continued chatting away. "When me was a bwoy, I t'ink I was a bwoy one time, no, a man, mi a donkey, cow and jackass. No, I was hog, pig or goat."

Grandma Hazel stopped talking. She only kept looking at Ody and shaking her head most of the time. "Poor t'ing," she mumbled. She could tell that his mental lights were burning dim. Ody was falling asleep and Grandma Hazel was ready to continue her journey. She said goodbye to Ody. "Walk good," he said. Finally Grandma Hazel reached the police station. She bent over her stick, while wiping her sweaty face with her apron. A tall, slender, middle-aged officer greeted Grandma Hazel at the door. His handsome looks were worthy of consideration. "My name is Officer Quay." He stretched his right hand out, offering Grandma Hazel a handshake. "What may I do for you today?" he politely asked.

"Notin!" she shouted breathlessly, stepping backwards as she placed her hand behind her in resentment.

The officer smiled. "I would never hurt you dear." He shook his head pitiably, placing his right hand on his chest.

"Weh de two policeman mi hear seh married? Is you?" Grandma Hazel asked in a querulous voice. "Yes a yuh!" She continued, answering her own question before the officer could respond. "A t'ink Timothy call one name like you, Quaty Case or whatever is yuh name."

Officer Quay stood looking and listening; he was anxious to help Grandma Hazel, but he had no idea what she was talking about. He was recently married and transferred to this location only two days ago. "I just got married," he replied, his face brightening with a joyous smile. "I would be more than happy to introduce you to my wife one day."

"Yuh wife!" Grandma Hazel shouted, raising her stick at the officer while hobbling in her gait. With one unsteady blow she hit the officer on his shoulder, incidentally shattering the glass window. Her unsteady gait caused her to stumble and fall. Grandma Hazel shouted, "Help! Help!"

Officer Quay grabbed on to Grandma Hazel, preventing her from knocking over the bench onto her small frame. Another officer came running to see what was happening. "Help! Help!" Grandma Hazel again shouted.

Officer Tubi stepped briskly on the creaking wooden floors.

He looked at Officer Quay with a terrified inquiry in his eyes. "What are you doing to that poor old lady?" he asked while pulling the officer's hand from off Grandma Hazel. "We do not brutalize old people here! You savage!" he shouted angrily, his eyes fixed directly on Officer Quay.

"I-I-I-I," stammered Officer Quay, the words frozen in his mouth. Before his words could defrost so he could try to defend himself, the chief who was well known to make drastic decisions, suspended him from duty temporarily.

Officer Quay was shaking with fear. The innocent, frightened officer hurriedly got into his car, angrily slamming the door. "Ouch! Oooo! Wooh! Wooh! Mercy! Mi finga! Lawd! Oooh!" Officer Quay held his hand between his thighs, pressing down as hard as he could. "Dat crosses son of a gun lawd! Lawd! What mi come a dis bush fah?" He groaned loudly.

Officer Tubi overheard the loud noise and walked down to where Officer Quay's car was parked. Without noticing what had happened, he shouted angrily at Officer Quay, "Listen man! A how de hell yuh get inna de police force eh? De recruiting officer a mussi yuh grampa. A big man like you, I just barely talk to yuh and yuh sit in yuh car crying like a spoiled child. Get outa de police force and follow yuh mada go a river go wash clothes to backfoot. Anyway when mosquito bite yuh, maybe yuh will run and cry. Get off a de govament property boss!" He waved his hand in disgust. Officer Tubi walked away talking to himself. "Blinking jackass, I don't know why dem send such a wimp up here fa. He should never be in the force at all."

Officer Quay sat in his car, pressing his hand down on the seat, rocking backwards and forwards as he grimaced in pain. His finger had a dent to the mid joint and was swollen twice its normal size. He decided to drive to the health clinic.

Upon bending the deep corner about two miles from the clinic, a little old lady stood at the corner of the road indicating her need for a drive. Office Quay took a short glimpse at the lady who looked as if she would crumble at a touch. He hissed his teeth. "Old crosses," he muttered. "Everything cause from dat crosses old woman." He drove past her, looking straight ahead, trying not to look at her. He had a conscience about his unkind action and he slowed down, stopped and put the car in reverse. The old lady walked slowly to the car. "Howdy sah, yuh a pass up a de clinic caa gi mi a drop? Lawd de heat deh kill mi," she said. Sweat was dripping off her face. Her hand seemed too weak to open the door. Officer Quay's hand was hurting badly. He had to get out of the car in order to use his right hand to open the door. She sat in the front seat. "T'ank yuh sar," she said, looking at him pleasingly. "A see say yuh a police, no wanda yuh stop. Yuh know fram when mi stan up out ya!"

"I am going to the clinic myself," said Officer Quay.

"Oh, yuh a go pick up yuh wife?"

"No mam, I slammed the car door on my finger, it is badly swollen," he said, holding up his hand.

"Lawd, eh swell up eeh!" she said, looking surprised. "Buy de black Benjamin healing oil, an' rub up some guinea hen bush an' mix dem up, den put eh ena piece a cloth an' bandage de finga. As soon as yuh feel eh draw de finga couple time de swellin an' de infarmation wi go dung."

"I am afraid the bone is broken," Officer Quay replied.

"Oh God," she said in a pitying voice. "Mek mi knock board." She knocked on the glass window. "As ole as yuh see mi, mi neva bruk none a mi bone fra mi baan. Once yuh bone bruk a de joint yuh get hautritis an' de pain no tap yasso. Fi mi gramma, God res' her soul, she go inna her grave a bawl fi pain fram hautritis."

Officer Quay looked at the old lady, his face pinched with pain. "So they buried her alive," he said, masking his pain with a smile.

"No sah, ha ha ha!" she laughed. "No sah, mi no mean eh like dat sah, mi know yuh a pull mi leg." They arrived at the clinic. "What is yuh name sah?" the old lady asked.

"Officer Quay," he replied.

"Nice to meet yuh sah, my name is Sisiline, dem call mi Sissy. T'ank yuh sah, God bless yuh!"

"My pleasure," said Officer Quay as he helped her out of the car.

"Wooh," she said, brushing her skirt hem down and limping towards the door. "Lawd mi poor ole foot pain up."

Officer Quay walked towards the door of the clinic. A security guard stood in the middle of the doorway looking like someone whom age had shown no mercy. His mouth was set in ugly lines of discontentment. He had a sulphur and molasses complexion. Walking towards the officer with his chest distended like a pouter pigeon he asked, "What can I do for you officer?"

Officer Quay took his cap off and held his wounded hand up. "I slammed my car door on my hand, seems like the bone is broken," he said.

"If you can slam your own finger in your car door, what would you do with mine? Yuh maybe woulda chop eh off. We not taking anybody else for the day, yuh haffi go up a de hospital."

"Can't you just take one more?" Officer Quay asked.

"Read my lips," the security guard said. "No!" As the officer turned to walk away, a young nurse walked to the door, swaying her hips. She was flamboyantly shaped. Her limbs were fit to serve as a sculptor's model and her lips demanded the consolation of a kiss. "What does the officer want?" she asked.

"Say him slam him han' in a car door," replied the guard.

"Oh no!" she said, her face saddened. She walked briskly towards Officer Quay. "Let me see your hand." She looked at his hand with care and concern. "We have stopped taking people in for the day but walk to the back door and I will let you in. Don't let anyone see you or we will have trouble here." Officer Quay sneaked his way to the back door. She examined his hand. "I can only give you something for the pain, put your arm in a sling and you will have to go to the emergency room at the hospital. They will do an X-ray to see if your bone is broken. They are on go slow up there, but I will call Nurse Sawyer, she is very nice. She will take care of you. I can imagine the pain."

"Thank you Nurse, I appreciate your kindness," said Officer Quay who although in pain, was looking at the nurse as if he had something else to say.

"Remember now, ask for Nurse Sawyer and tell her Nurse Cobalt sent you." Officer Quay nodded and walked away, wondering how he would be able to drive with one arm in a sling. As he was walking back to his car, a voice from the far corner of the waiting area was heard.

"Babylon bruk him han' to backfoot. Peanut an' suck-suck, peanut an' suck-suck mi a sell." A young man was walking around the clinic selling snacks.

"A fra when oonuh sidung out ya?" he asked the group.

"Rasta, dem seh dem na tek nobody else," answered a young man who was bleeding from a wound on his leg.

"A wicked dem wicked, fiah gwine bun dem up! Nuh dem tek de babylon tru de back door ana tek care a him," said the young man.

"Oh, a dat why mi see de lilly maga nurse a talk to him, she hide an' let him in, yuh see how dem stay," said a lady in the group.

"A musa her relative," said another lady.

"No, a musa look she a look him," another voice chimed in.

"Look him? She maybe have him already," one said, putting in her two cents.

"She look half starve," said another woman who was eating a beef patty and gulping down soda from a can as if she only had one minute to live. "Even one old woman dem turn back, she say she have presha. De poor ole woman musa drop dung a road," said a middle-aged woman, who tied her head with a red scarf. She had pencils sticking out on both sides. She was wearing a white robe and had sweat dripping from all over as if she was jumping at a revival. "Oonuh no see seh class prejudice rule Jamdung."

"A because a babylon man. Hey sista, buy one a mi sky-juice, cool dung yuh tempa nuh," said the young man to another lady who was swearing and making threats.

"Galang bout yuh business rasta, weh mi fi get money from?" she asked.

"A ristocratic looking dawta like yuh nuh ha money? Deal wid mi no lady," he said.

"Yuh t'ink mi cah live inna sky-juice cone? Gwaan bout yuh business rasta, wha money mi have no enough fi pay mi rent," said the woman. "Sell soma dem big rope gole chain yuh have roun' yuh neck a bruk yuh neck an' a bline mi eye."

"Yuh can come live wid mi yuh nuh dawta."

"A musa inna yuh sky-juice cart yuh live, mi caa hole in deh," replied the woman, who was serious as a corpse. The group burst out in laughter. The young man went his way pushing his cart and calling out "Peanut and sky-juice!" and making mischievous comments as he walked around.

Officer Quay arrived at the hospital. People milled around everywhere and hospital workers in various coloured uniforms were standing in groups chattering away, some shouting "Strike! Strike! Go-slow! Go-slow!" Some held up cardboard signs, cloth flags marked 'Go-slow' and 'Underpaid and Overworked'. Officer Quay slowly stepped out of his car. His face was sour, wearing an expression of pain and disappointment. Someone shouted from under a shade tree, "Babylon, dem bruk up yuh han'!" Officer Quay held his head straight as he walked up to the emergency room door. The grilled door was closed and surrounded by police officers and security guards. There was a large crowd; some were pushing their way through the crowd and fights and quarrels broke out momentarily. A few persons fainted from the heat and sickness. Loud sirens and flashing lights from ambulances and police cars could be seen and heard. The outburst of crying and moaning was hard to bear. People were coming from far and near with head injuries, broken bones, burns, stab wounds and ailments of all descriptions. Officer Quay thought, If I had taken the sling off, I could have easily got through this crowd. I could pretend I was on duty and who would know? I could be on light duty with my arm in a sling. He recognized one of his colleagues from the station where he was, prior to his transfer.

He walked up to him.

"What happened to your arm since you just transfer the other day man? No tell mi say yuh mek de country bwoy dem bad-man yuh off."

"No a slam mi slam it inna de confounded car door boss," he replied.

"How yuh get fi do dat man? A what you had on your mind? Nuh tell mi since yuh jus married yuh having problems already."

"No, yuh know, a me and de chief up ah de station had some problem because of a little disturbed old woman. No fault of mine boss, just some misunderstanding. He is so hot tempered that 'im even dismiss mi from duty temporarily, but call mi later boss. I am here to see a special nurse."

"Hold on boss, stay right here, let mi go break up dat fight ova deh so." Officer Burket walked briskly over to where two women were brutally hitting each other with the heel of their shoes. One woman complained that she had an emergency and was aggravated by the woman who was talking too loudly on her phone. People were rushing to the scene swearing, laughing and shouting. None would attempt to break up the fight due to fear of getting hit too. Officer Burket could only disperse the crowd by threatening to use tear gas. Officer Burket walked back to where Officer Quay was waiting.

"Hear mi boss, yuh see how the crowd angry and everything getting outa hand, let me go and get her for you. In this way dem caa seh we let yuh in because some a dem is here from before daylight dis morning. What is the nurse name?"

"Aam, aam, oh, Nurse Cobalt. No, Nurse Cobalt send me to see Nurse Sawyer," replied Officer Quay.

"Alright, stay right here boss," said Officer Burket.

A middle aged nurse walked to the door, she had the perfect appearance of an overworked emergency room nurse. Her cap stood on her forehead as if too tired of sitting in the same spot. The heels of her shoes leaned in the direction of the door as if saying they were ready to go home. Her teeth were milky white but stood apart as though they were upset with each other. She was buffing sweat from her face and fanning herself. "This is Nurse Sawyer. Are you here to arrest me Officer?" she asked, smiling.

"No, I can only use one arm," Officer Quay replied, returning her smile.

"Come with me," she said. "You can have a seat here, I will be with you in a few minutes." She walked back to the young man to whom she was attending. He was making a loud noise, screaming and swearing, due to the pain from a gunshot wound.

"If you continue screaming in my ears, I will leave you here and take care of someone else. You are not the only one here who is hurting," said Nurse Sawyer.

"What yuh going to do Nurse, lef' mi go tek care a de beas' ova dere?" the young man asked anxiously. "Fiah fi de babylon!" he shouted. "Fiah bun dung babylon!"

"Yuh a mad man?" the nurse asked. "Stop the noise in my ears."

"A no mi mad, a de policeman ova dere, look how much cow vehicle a knock dung a road. Instead a 'im pick up one throw inna im jeep carry home go cook, an' mek cow cod soup put strent inna him, 'im mek tief wrestle him an' bruk him han'. A weak bwoy dat. A one a dem shot me inna mi leg. Fiah fi de babylon! Brimstone an' fiah, bun up de babylon! Fiah fi yuh!"

The security guard walked over to his stretcher. "Listen man, if yuh no shut up yuh mouth, yuh going haffi go back a yuh yard widout care, yuh lucky yuh in here, we on go-slow."

"Nutting new iah, oonuh on go-slow every day, oonuh only a go slower today. A 'go-slower' oonuh on, bout go-slow," the young man replied, hissing his teeth and swearing. The guard walked away shaking his head. Nurse Sawyer assigned a student nurse to take care of Officer Quay while she attended to a patient with third degree burns. Nurse Acton tried to examine Officer Quay's hand prior to sending him for an X-ray.

"Oh! Oooh!" Officer Quay cried.

"Babylon a bawl like baby. Why de security bwoy no tell 'im fi shut up? Fiah fi all a oonuh! Jah! Rastafari! King a Babylon, Rula of Zion!" he shouted.

Two warders came and took the young man to the X-ray department. "Do not go down there with your noise," Nurse Sawyer warned, giving him a stern look. "There are other patients there, some elderly who cannot tolerate noise."

"Pain no ha no respect iah," he replied. "Peace Nursey," he said, holding up two fingers as the warders pulled the stretcher. "Ouch!" he shouted as the warders pulled the stretcher over a bump. "Tek time no boss."

"The amount a mout' yuh have," the warders replied as they pulled the stretcher faster.

"Sorry rasta, mi waa go a mi yaad," the security guard said, "we caa tek what we nuh have, no have no time fi tek time."

....

Officer Tubi hurried to get back to Grandma Hazel, who was about to go through the door. He helped her to a chair. "My name is Officer Tubi. Please accept my apology dear lady," he said. "Have you been hurt in anyway?" He held Grandma Hazel's hands together, his face marked with pity.

Grandma Hazel quickly pulled her hands away, her eyes staring wildly. "Jesus have mercy!" she shouted. "Dear God!"

The officer quickly let go of Grandma Hazel's hands, not knowing why she was pulling her hands away.

"Oh, my God! Your hands are hurting, seems as if he hurt your hand. Please sit right here Grandma, I will get you something to drink, then take you to the clinic up the road."

"No sah," said Grandma Hazel, shaking her head. "Not if me dying sah. My God!"

"Ok, what I will do is put some ice on your hand then take you to the nurse at the clinic," Officer Tubi said.

"No, no, no sah, I will catch up cole sah. Mi han' not hurting bad sah, when me go home me will rub it wid tiger balm an' tie de gunea hen bush on it sah."

"Ok Grandma, what is your real name?"

"Me sah?" she asked. Her mind was preoccupied, thinking how the name Tubi sounded like the name Timothy mentioned earlier, and also how she was mistaken with the officer whom she assaulted.

After a moment of hesitation she said, "My name is Hazel Barlon."

"You are a brave lady," the officer said, smiling. "What brought you here?"

"My two weak shakey legs an' mi walking stick an' de mercy of God," she replied.

Officer Tubi shook his head, took his glasses off and laid it on the desk. He walked over to the area where the other officers were playing dominoes.

"We have a confused old lady here, I have to make arrangements to take her home," he said.

"Good luck," replied one of the officers as they continued playing their domino game.

Officer Tubi returned and took a seat closer to Grandma Hazel.

"So your name is Hazel Barlon..."

"Everybody call me Grandma Hazel," she replied. She became uncomfortable with the officer sitting so close to her. She started to shuffle and move further down on the wooden bench.

"Do you know your address?" the officer asked.

"No t'ank yuh sah, I don't need no more dress sah, my dawta sen' whole heap a frock from Merica fi mi sah, but mi no wear dem sah, I put dem up. All whole heap a nightie an' bed tings, I put dem up in de grip an' de trunk."

"Why don't you wear your clothes that your daughter send for you?"

"I put dem down fi sickness sah, far when yuh sick an' de fass people dem come look fi yuh dem only come to see what yuh place look like an' what dem can get fi t'ief. Den dem carry yuh business pon light pose go chat."

Officer Tubi looked confused but kept a smile on his face.

"Grandma, where do you live?" he asked.

"Down de hill an' far ova de road sah."

"Why did you stop here?" he asked.

"Stop here, oh!" replied Grandma Hazel, her face startled. "Somet'ing mi did wah fi find out."

Officer Tubi moved closer to her, listening attentively.

"One policeman up here name, aam, aam - tapping her fingers on the desk - oh gosh, - tapping louder - him name start with Q."

"You mean Quay? That's the officer who was unkind to you? His name is Quay Wheelright."

"Him married sah?" Grandma Hazel asked.

"Oh yes, he recently married a lovely young lady," said Officer Tubi.

"Young woman, young lady?" she repeated, looking at the officer quizzically. Her mouth hung open. "Oh my God, poor t'ing," she whispered under her breath.

"What's wrong Grandma?"

She snapped back into herself. "Not a t'ing, not a t'ing sah!" she replied. "Where your wife is?"

"Oh," Officer Tubi said, raising his eyebrows which were hanging like tuffs of dry grass. "She is at work, she teaches at the high school. She, she..."

"What is her name?" Grandma Hazel asked. Officer Tubi gave a guilt-filled look. Just then, another officer walked by and heard the conversation. Officer Tubi answered and immediately walked away to avoid any other question. He did not have the least idea what Grandma Hazel was thinking but did not want the other officer to hear since he was aware of his relationship. Grandma Hazel was thinking deeply. She mumbled, "Questron, questron, Timothy say ques something." She looked all around then grabbed her stick and tried to walk quietly through the door. She hobbled down the flight of concrete steps. Grandma Hazel looked up at the clouds, hoping there was no rain on the horizon.

It was sunset. The sky was orange and gold at one corner with white clouds surrounding it like a 'sunny - side - up' egg. She contemplated the long journey home. Her aged joints ached from the thought. "I must hurry before dusk an' I caa see good. If I did know I was going to stay so long, I would carry mi bottle lamp," she said as she walked down the road .

Officer Tubi rushed into his Ford pick-up truck trying to catch up with Grandma Hazel. She looked behind her and saw the vehicle. Recognizing that it was a police vehicle, she muttered, "A hope a nuh dat blinking mad man what married to man, 'im haffi blinking mad fi do dat."

The truck stopped, sending a cloud of dust in the air.

"Grandma, why did you walk away? I intended to take you home. I could never allow you to walk home," Officer Tubi said. "Grandma, you nuh easy at all. You are indeed a brave lady but it is too late and it will be dark soon. It is dangerous to be walking by yourself at this time."

Grandma Hazel was quiet for a while. She thought of her aching legs and the long journey home. She said, "Dem seh drowning man catch on to straw." Officer Tubi helped her into his truck and drove off down the road.

The grey clouds were moving slowly across the sky. The wild flowers along the road bowed their heads to sleep. Night was drawing nigh. Timothy saw the fowls going to roost.

"Grandma never take such a long nap, she always count the fowls when they are going to roost. Wonders never cease," he said, bowing his head to think. "No, something has to be wrong with her."

"She may be just tired," Lorna said.

"Mom, grandma never sleep so long," said Timothy. "Come, let's check up on her," Lorna said, and they walked briskly indoors to see Grandma Hazel.

Grandma Hazel had gotten close to home. She pointed to a house a few yards away.

"Sah, a beg yuh stop at de house wid de two drum pan in front."

She was busy thinking how to get into the house without Lorna and Timothy seeing her. She said, "T'anks officer. Drive back safe sah."

"I will wait until you get inside," he said.

"No sah, see dem looking out through de window fi mi, alright sah." Grandma Hazel pretended to be wiping her face. As soon as the truck was out of sight, she walked to her house.

By this time, Lorna and Timothy ran into Grandma Hazel at the door. Dreary disappointment was printed on Grandma Hazel's face. "Grandma!" Lorna shouted, startled at seeing her. "Where were you? You look tired, we thought you were sleeping."

"No, I walk dung de road," she replied, walking past Lorna and Timothy.

"You never stayed out so late," Timothy said.

"Bwoy yuh no know how de people dung a road chatty chatty," said Grandma Hazel.

"They must have been talking about something interesting. You never let the fowl dem go to roost without you count them. What nuh happen in a year happen in a day," said Timothy.

"Grandma, yuh find a boyfriend?" Lorna asked, laughing and pinching Grandma Hazel on her cheeks. They were still rosy looking.

"Girout gal, yuh t'ink mi an' yuh a size? Dat all deh pan fi yuh head. Inna fi mi days nobody kno' wah yuh look like till yuh find a male companion an' married," Grandma Hazel said.

"Den Grandma, oonuh no touch-up touch-up?" Timothy asked, laughing and taking side steps while singing, "Grandma have a boyfriend!"

"You have to start dressing up in your new clothes," said Lorna.

"And you have to wear low rider pants Grandma," added Timothy.

Grandma Hazel hit at Timothy with her stick. "Yuh t'ink mi an' yuh a size bwoy? No mek mi hit yuh bat bat wid mi stick. Inna fi mi days we nuh inna no touch-up touch-up, or we nuh act fool fool like oonuh new generation. We married an' get straight to business an' have we children, an' if de man caa pay fi de marriage 'im no ready fi married yet. 'Im had to have a job or something."

"Alright Grandma a whole heap a years no business no happen," Lorna said laughing. "If yuh find a boyfriend yuh have to buy a bottle of WD40 fi pull that lock."

"Oonuh neida hab lock nor key, oonuh gallang some where else go chat oonuh slackness," Grandma Hazel said, walking away and brushing her hand behind her in disgust. "All de fowl dem gone on roose?"

"I don't know Grandma," replied Timothy.

"If tomorrow I miss one fedda much more one fowl yuh will get WD Hundred on yuh back wid mi supple jack. All oonuh know fe do a chat slackness."

"Get modern Grandma, time for a change," Timothy said.

CHAPTER Three

There was a loud banging on the gate. Timothy peeped through the window. A bright flame from a bottle torch could be seen, illuminating an old couple as they walked slowly through the gate. The old lady was pathetically bent, her chest almost touching the ground. She was leaning on her stick and peering over her glasses.

A thin-bodied figure was walking behind her. Timothy recognized the couple and ran to assist them.

"Grandma is sitting in the hall, go in," Timothy told them. They looked at Grandma Hazel compassionately.

"What happen Hay Hay?"

"Come in mi dear Miss Dassa. Sit here Maas Freddie. You sit down on de three foot stool but no mek it break wid yuh." Maas Freddie moved as if his limbs were borrowed from death. Grandma Hazel told Lorna to get some coffee ready and asked Timothy to get some peppermint bush. The house she showed the police officer was really Miss Dassa and Maas Freddie's. They had seen her and came to find out what had happened.

"Lawd, mi never know a so de police dem nice," Grandma Hazel whispered. "Mi go for a walk up de road an' mi sit down under de big bassida tree fi catch mi breat. De officer come sidung beside mi. 'Im offer mi wata an' was talking to me. Den 'im ask mi if I want a drive home. Mi glad yuh see because de foot dem hurt an' stiff when mi walk. Mi did sorta fraid at firs' but den 'im strap mi down in de jeep. Mi mek 'im drop mi a your gate because mi neva want dem pickney ketch dem fraid t'ink a something happen to mi. Dem say 'im a dem man-woman but 'im no act like 'im mad and 'im very nice."

"He is a kine officer," Maas Freddie added. "Wi si when you come out a de jeep at wi gate. Wi wasa wanda wha happen, so wi seh mek wi come si. When wi reach a de deap corna de Maas Cogan mad son breeze pass we an' den turn back an' ask wi a weh wi going if wi want 'im fi walk wid wi. I fraida de bwoy so till mi bone dem start rackle. Mi tell 'im a ova de shop we going, so 'im start run again. Lawd ma, yuh coulda neva mek dat deh mad bwoy come near yuh, when 'im get off a 'im head a only stiff jacket can hole 'im."

"Stiff jacket, what is that?" Timothy asked, as he handed the peppermint to Lorna.

"Stiff jacket is a t'ick cloak what dem mek fi put on mad people," Maas Freddie replied.

"What stiff jacket do to mad people?" Timothy asked.

"De jacket keep dem stiff so come de name stiff jacket. Dem pull it up ova dem han', so dat dem two han' stay straight at dem side. De jacket don't ha nuh sleeve, it light an' it zip from bottom to top. Sometimes de police dem walk wid dem go to lock-up an' when de journey too far dem use buggy or what eva dem can get," Maas Freddie explained.

"Those were horrible days," said Lorna as she walked back to the outdoor kitchen. Lorna came back with an extremely black kettle that only knew wood fire and coal stove as Grandma Hazel refused to have gas or electricity around her. The coffee was steaming hot, its appetizing aroma could be smelt from far away. Lorna placed three mugs on the long wooden bench and poured the coffee. She gave Grandma Hazel a special mug with mint tea then served coffee to Maas Freddie and Miss Dassa. "Lorna how many times mi mus' tell yuh seh when yuh serving outside people, yuh mus' use de waita?" Grandma Hazel asked furiously.

"Waiter? Waiter work in restaurant and bar Grandma, it's called tray," Lorna replied.

"Too much a yuh mouth! What yuh fi kno' you nuh kno'," Grandma Hazel replied angrily.

"A waiter wi call it inna fi wi days an' dem look de same up to now," Miss Dassa said.

"So what did you call the people who worked and served in restaurants and bars?" Timothy asked.

"Maid an' bar maid we use to call dem. A matter of fact wi only ha one or two cookshop. People mostly use dem house an' when it come to bar, is only de owner in dere an' dem live same place," said Maas Freddie.

"Interesting, I want to hear more about stiff jacket," said Lorna, as she went to fetch the tray.

Everyone sat comfortably on the verandah. The bottle torch was burning brightly, sending black smoke and strong oily fumes into the clean night air. As soon as the light became dim, Maas Freddie tilted the bottle, allowing kerosene oil to soak the paper cork. The flames gushed up suddenly then slowly went down. The little brown bugs called 'may bug' or 'parch corn' due to their rough, crisp outer covering, were flying around the light. Some fell on the floor and even in the coffee mugs. Maas Freddie kept fanning them with his cap, avoiding them dropping in his coffee. When a few did, he poured a little coffee out with the bugs and continued drinking. The little bugs with beautiful green lights called 'winka' were flying around. The peenie wallie with their bright amber lights flew amidst them, also illuminating the dark night.

"Alright, back to the stiff jacket," said Lorna. Maas Freddie took a long sip of his coffee, which sounded as if he was sucking conch from its shell. One could stay a mile away and hear the big belch. Maas Freddie hit his chest loudly then made another huge belch. "T'ank God, mannas," he said. "De coffee always get ridda de gas."

"No Maas Freddie," said Timothy. "The coffee gives you gas and your stomach gets rid of it."

"Mi nuh care," said Maas Freddie. "As long as it come out. Inna fi mi days different from today days. When people get off a dem head, de police man haffi put stiff jacket pan dem because dem kick, buck an' lick. You know it fava seh when dem mad dem stronga dan any time else. Eida dem walk wid dem go a madhouse or borrow horse an' cart an' carry dem in dere."

"Poor Miss Jamie dead an' gone. God res' her soul. A salt dem use to tie on fi her head an' it neva stop de madness. All now nobody know what happen to her," Grandma Hazel said. "She use to mad so tell, when yuh ask Miss Jamie what is her name, she tell yuh ten different name what no written in de Lamb Book of Life. An' she use to ketch her own pee-pee in butta pan an' drink it say is rain wata. Worse of all, she use to ketch lizard put inna sardine can, throw vinegar on it an' eat it seh is sardine, dem haffi put her weh fas' fas'."

"Mi hear seh she did get betta an' dem carry her home to her poor mada but she nuh tek her back," said Maas Freddie.

"Why?" Timothy asked.

"No fraid dem fraid a her. Once yuh mad everybody fraid a yuh even if yuh nuh mad no more."

"Tell him Maas Freddie," Grandma Hazel said, looking at Timothy woefully.

Maas Freddie continued, "So den, dem carry her to her poor grandmother, she sorry fi her an' tek her in. It bring one hell in de district. She no act like she mad anymore but de people dem fraid a her. Some a dem put up fence wall an' baab wire round dem yaad, some buy dog. In no time she run mad again because de bwoy dem in de district give her ganja. She nearly kill de poor ole lady. She try fi run through de coffee walk one of de time when she threaten fi kill her. She drop an' bruk her waise."

"Hip Maas Freddie, is hip it name sah," Timothy said.

"Afta yuh neva born yet, how yuh know?" Maas Freddie asked.

"Shut up Timothy," Lorna interrupted.

Maas Freddie continued. "She stay inna haspital fi bout six munt. Dem tie her up inna iron an' cord like when chokie ketch bud."

"Ha ha ha ha," Timothy laughed. "It name traction Maas Freddie."

"Fraction, action all de same," Grandma Hazel said.

"Dem feed her on porridge everyday. When she come outa hospital, she maga so till she look like when smady ha consumption. Dem haffi feed her pan molasses like when dem a fatten hog fi kill," said Maas Freddie.

"How comes dem use to keep people so long in the

hospital?" Lorna asked.

Maas Freddie held the coffee mug above his mouth, draining the last drop of coffee and making an unbearable sound as if he wanted to suck the entire mug in his stomach. He wiped his mouth with his hand then continued talking. "Dem never ha all de t'ings wha dem ha now inna fi wi days."

"Mi dear sah, dem ya new generation live inna paradise compare to fi wi days," said Grandma Hazel.

Timothy poured more coffee in Maas Freddie's mug, while winking to his mother. "Maas Freddie, Maas Freddie tell us more about old time days," Timothy begged, taking a seat close to him. He looked down at Maas Freddie's shoes. "I like your shoes Maas Freddie."

"A mi son cah dis from town fi mi, some new, some ole. Mi put up de new one dem, an' wear de ole one," said Maas Freddie, as he filled his pipe with tobacco.

"Nike shoes are expensive," Timothy said.

"Who name Niki, a Niki Maas Freddie son name?" Grandma Hazel asked.

Timothy and Lorna laughed. "No one Grandma," Lorna replied, patting Grandma Hazel on her shoulder.

"Poor mi gal," Grandma Hazel said as she elevated her legs on a small stool.

Maas Freddie lit his pipe, cleared his throat, then took a puff. The unpleasant, powerful scent of tobacco filled the air. Maas Freddie began. "When mi was a bwoy I get mi firs' pair a shoes when I was nine ears ole, mi caa figet, a glad so till ah sleep wid it unda mi pilla an' when mi wake up mi tie de lace roun' mi neck an' carry it wid mi ebry weh mi go. When rain fall, mi tek eh off an' carry it inna paper bag. Yuh see, certain time a year de school inspecta dem come roun' fi see what we a learn. Dem time deh, de teacha dem couldn't beat wi. Dem hide de strap an' de cane, yes sah, dem treat wi nice but when dem gone, wi back inna fiah again. Mi daddy use to grow hog an' goat an' mi mada haffi teaf one a de pig an' sell when mi daddy gone a Cave Valley gone sell food. She buy one pair a brown 'god bline mi' fi me, an' a pair a 'pussboot' fi mi sista."

"God what? Puss what?" Timothy and Lorna asked simultaneously, both laughing hysterically.

"It have a big roun' circle ova de ankle an' mek out a canvas. It lace up from de toe to above de ankle. De pussboot name crepe. It mek out a canvas to but dem call it pussboot because it no mek no soun' when yuh walk."

Grandma Hazel said, "Fi mi firs' shoes was a brown crepe, de same pussboot what Maas Freddie was talking about. Is when mi a big gal de church was having a big concert. People from all ova de globe was coming an' mi did ha to seh a recitation, so mi granmada sell one acre a lan fi one guinea."

"One guinea? One guinea?" Timothy repeated.

"Dat was twenty-one shilling," Grandma Hazel said.

"Timothy you know that Jamaica was ruled under the British. The currency was pound, shilling and pence just like England," said Lorna.

"Yes Mom, I heard about pound, shilling and pence, but not guinea," Timothy replied.

"Lawd dem time deh was hard time. Most people walk barefoot. Wi wash wi foot clean, rub it wid coconut oil from top to bottom. We foot an' han' an' face shine an' clean," Grandma Hazel said.

"Shine?" Lorna asked. "Oh boy. What was the sense of washing your feet then put it back in the dirt? By the time you start walking your feet get dirty again."

"Well, dat is how t'ings was dem time deh," said Grandma

Hazel. "My second shoes was a 'mash potato'."

Timothy laughed until he fell off the stool.

"Bwoy if yuh eva mash up mi stool, mi nuh know how mi an' yuh would mek it."

"Grandma remember mama bought you two nice chairs," said Lorna.

"Yes, mek dem stay fi tek shame outa mi eye later when mi sick."

"Grandma can you describe 'mash potato' shoes to me?" Lorna asked.

"I will never forget," said Grandma Hazel. "It was brown, mek out of plastic, de back open, backless an' toeless an' mek wid some little hole fi air or wata go trough. Two t'ings bout dem, when rain fall, dem tek in so much wata mi foot slide slide in an' outa dem. If yuh nuh mine sharp yuh bruk yuh ankle. When sun hot it burn mi foot so tell mi haffi tek it off."

"Why did they call it mash potato?" Lorna asked.

Miss Dassa awoke from her nap, heard the conversation and hissed her gum in disgust. She was practically toothless. "Oonuh young generation no ha no common sense," she said. "Dem call it mash potato because when sun hot it bun yuh foot like hot mash potata."

"No," said Maas Freddie. "Dem call it mash potata because people use to like wear dem go a dance an' dem move dem foot to de music like when yuh a mash potata." Maas Freddie tried to show them how they danced but he clanked like a worn out machine in motion.

"Sidung!" Miss Dassa shouted. "Next t'ing yuh drap bruk yuh bone an' end up inna hospital inna fraction like poor Chiquita."

Timothy giggled and said, "Traction Miss Dassa."

"What de difference?" she asked.

"The T the F," Timothy answered, laughing.

Maas Freddie said, "Oh oo" as his little beady eyes widened in recognition. "Mi see dem lilly pickney inna Mr. Brown shop a wear dem sometime."

"Oh, that is how they look," said Lorna.

"Same so, same so. Only seh de mash potato neva so tin an' shine an' dem neva ha dem deh bright cola deh. A only black an' brown dem use to ha."

"Fred yuh memba wha kina trouses dem use to wear wid de 'god bline mi,' go a school?" Miss Dassa asked.

"Nuh trouses," he replied.

"Wha kine?" Miss Dassa asked.

"Trouses, trouses wid suspenda fi keep it up," said Maas Freddie.

"A no dat mi mean. A three quata drape dem use to wear. It look like wha dem young gal a wear now," said Miss Dassa.

Lorna ran inside to fetch one of her Capri pants. She held it up and asked, "Like this?"

"Yes, yes but it neva mek so fancy wid all dem shiney shiney roun' de foot."

"Sequin Miss Dassa," Timothy said.

"Bwoy shet yuh mouth, who care if a sea queen or sea king dem call it," said Miss Dassa.

"So wha bout the pedal pusha an' de drain pipe?" Grandma Hazel asked.

Timothy and Lorna looked at each other. "Drain pipe?" Lorna asked, her face masked with an incredulous look.

"Yes drain pipe," Grandma Hazel replied. "Firs' it was pedal pusher because people use to wear dem mostly when dem ridin' bicycle because it was easier fi push de pedal an de foot nuh catch in de bicycle chain. Afta dat, a new style come in name drain pipe. Dem mek de foot dem narrow at de bottom, so now it name crockery."

Lorna laughed. "Grandma, it is called capri."

"Den what yuh t'ink we use to write on a school?" Grandma Hazel asked.

"Slate," Miss Dassa replied. "Infant school pickney use slate, some still deh bout de place but de funny t'ing, our slate use to ha John Crow bead on it so we could learn fi count."

"These now have beads but not crow beads," Lorna said.

"Were the beads made from John Crow eyes or what?" Timothy asked.

"No, dem call it John Crow bead because dem red like John Crow head. Dem grow on tree an' den when dem dry, dem bore hole in dem an' run wire trough dem," Grandma Hazel replied. "When de slate drop it break an' wi parents beat wi. Wi have to use de piece till end a year when wi parents sell coffee or animal, wi get a new slate. Some af dem bore hole in de slate frame, wax cord put in de slate frame an' let wi put it roun' wi neck."

"What if yuh fall?" Timothy asked.

"Yuh betta nuh fall dung, yuh get beaten if de slate break. Who care if yuh fall dung, as long as de slate nuh break."

Lorna's mouth fell open with a frightened droop.

"Well hear dis," Maas Freddie said. "Worse dan dat, some people break one slate in four piece fi serve four pickney.

It was hard fi fine four shilling to buy four slate. Den one slate pencil break inna four piece. Yuh could hardly hold it fi write. Wi write an' rub it out wid cloth or wata."

"So did you have to keep running to the tap for water to clean your slate during class time?" Timothy asked.

"No, mose of de time we spit on de slate an' rub it off wid wi han'."

Maas Freddie helped himself to another mug of coffee which seemed to help him stay awake and add wings to his tongue. He took a long, loud sip and looked at Lorna. "What yuh t'ink people use to drink from, especially when dem a work a bush? Wi use to have a tree name 'packey' tree, dem always bear some big roun' shine green looking t'ings like pear. De 'kin tough almost like coconut shell. Wi pick dem, an' cut dem roun' in two half. Wi clean out the pulp, wash dem clean, dry dem in de sun an' use dem as cup. Lawd dem keep de wata cool. Some people use dem mek music shaka. Wi cut green banana leaf an' quail it ova fire, dat is what wi use as plate."

"Why did you hold the leaf over fire? To kill the insects?" Lorna asked.

"No, to make sure the leaf no tear," Maas Freddie replied. "Wi use stick fi eat an' use de dry brown gauze from de coconut tree as strainer."

"That was dirty," Lorna said.

"No, no, wi wash dem clean. God provide everything an' de earth fi we use, wi neva haffi go a shop fi buy dem t'ings. Wi ketch rain wata, an' de funny t'ing, people neva so sick like today. Some kina sickness mi hear bout today, mi neva hear dem deh when mi was a young lad coming up. Even de docta no know what fi call it, so dem mek up one long name, if yuh try fi denounce it yuh jawbone bruk," Maas Freddie said.

"Pronounce, not denounce," Timothy corrected.

Maas Freddie hissed his lonely tooth. "Bwoy, a musa fi yuh pa write de word an' meaning book," he replied.

"Dictionary," Timothy corrected again.

"We cut tree, burn coal an' draw wood mek fire," said Miss Dassa.

"Mi still use mi coal an' wood," Grandma Hazel said. "No bady nat carrying no gas nor electricity stove come inna fi mi house." She looked directly at Lorna.

"How did you light the fire?" Timothy asked.

"Rub stone or metal togeda," Maas Freddie replied.

"How about clothes?" Lorna asked.

"Is leaf Adam an' Eve use mek clothes," Miss Dassa replied.

"They could not do any better," Lorna said.

Miss Dassa drained her coffee cup dry. "Dem time was de good ole time," she said, as she got up from her seat.

"Are you going home now Miss Dassa?" Lorna asked.

"No, mi nuh ready yet, mi wah pee-pee, mi going to stoop dung roun' a de house corner," she replied.

"No, Miss Dassa, yuh can't go back there, that is where all the tea bush dem grow," Timothy told her.

"Bwoy shet yuh mouth, pee-pee wi mek dem grow fas', a de best fertilizer," Miss Dassa replied.

"Fertilizer?" Timothy asked, giving a concerned look. "Me nat drinking your pee-pee ma, if you go back there, I am going to chop down all of them."

"Go wid her an' show her where to go. She caa piss pan mi tea bush, de acid from her piss will kill dem. So all this time when mi use to get spirit weed an' comfry bush from her, I neva know

seh is dem renkin piss mi use to drink. Have mercy my God!"
Grandma Hazel said, making a scornful facial expression.

"Come Miss Dassa, I will go with you," Lorna told her as
she fetched the bottle torch.

"What a relief," Miss Dassa said as they walked back to
the verandah.

"You can wash your hands here Miss Dassa." Lorna
dipped up some water from the water drum.

"Lawd, a only pee-pee mi pee-pee, mi han' nuh dirty,"
Miss Dassa said.

"It will not hurt," Lorna told her while she handed her
the soap and poured water onto her hands. Miss Dassa
dried her hands in her apron and sat down.

CHAPTER
Four

Lorna sat close to Miss Dassa. "So, Miss Dassa, you said Adam and Eve used leaf to make clothes in the Garden of Eden. We can't use leaf to make clothes so we would have to buy clothes."

"Some use to use flour bag an' crocus bag," Grandma Hazel interjected. "Wi wash de flour bag, bleach it in de sun till it white. After dat wi wash dem wid brown soap an' rinse dem in blue. Wi use dem to mek many different things from clothes to bed linen, even under wear. Wi embroidery dem at school. Dem use to pretty! Now a days generation would prefer walk naked dan go worry wid dem t'ings. Some a dem not even know fi string needle much more fi use timble. If shop an' store destroy from dis earth, dem would perish for dem nuh know fi turn dem han' an' make fashan."

"God provide everything real fi we use," Miss Dassa added.

"Ok Miss Dassa, if God provide everything real for us to use, where did you get soap from?" Timothy asked.

"Soap? Fi mi parents use to use ackee skin."

"Ackee skin? Ackee skin can wash clothes?" he asked.

"Bwoy shet yuh mouth, da sinting sud so till. It sud like any soap," Grandma Hazel added. "Well, mi know when mi was a pickney my granmada use it, an' mi use it. Mi still use mi scrubbing board up to now, but I don't use de ackee skin no more."

"So, you never use bleach?" Timothy asked.

"Bleach? No, wi put de clothes in de sun on zinc or rock, dat was enough bleach, an' all dem poisonous sinting oonuh deh draw up inna oonuh nose, wi neva use to sick-sick like oonuh. Wi use wi han' fi sew, some people hab han' machine."

"All now you use your hands Grandma," Timothy reminded her.

"Shut up Timothy, hand sewn clothes are expensive today," Lorna informed.

"Well, wi use to use wi han' dem because inna dose days wi couldn't afford machines," Grandma Hazel explained.

"How about telephones?" Lorna inquired.

"Ha, ha, ha telephone!" exclaimed Miss Dassa. "De only telephone mi hear bout dem time deh was when people use to use Betty condense milk can."

"To do what?" Timothy asked.

"To talk to one anedda. Dem knot one end a de cord den push de nex' end tru de nex' can, an' knot de end. De cord haffi be about two to tree chain long. Dem talk loud in one can, den put de nex' can at dem ears fi hear what de nex' one saying."

Timothy, looking astonished asked, "What you mean when you say two chains?"

"Twenty-two yard mek one chain so two chain a 44 yards."

"Grandma, it is not yard and chain anymore, it's meter and centimeter," Lorna informed her.

"Well, mi nuh know notin bout oonuh peta an' saint peta, afta is nat bible mi talking bout," Grandma Hazel replied. "Now a days as de pickney dem run or walk outa dem muma belly, dem seh 'Hello! Hello!' It look like dem born wid telephone a dem ears."

"No wanda now a days pickney hab running ears so much," Miss Dassa added.

"It's not running ears Miss Dassa. It is called ear infection," Lorna said.

"Shut up! She nuh care if a ear inna fraction or outa fraction, all de same," Grandma Hazel said.

"Grandma, Grandma I'm sure you had to buy pots," Timothy said.

"Wi neva haffi buy pot if wi nuh want fi buy it. Wi cook inna kerosene pan when is plenty people. Some people use cheese pan or butter pan. Wi wash de kerosene pan good an' turn it down on de ground for a while so dat de kerosene smell come out. Wi use to hab good tree leg iron pot, mi still hab one unda de house battam," Grandma Hazel replied.

"Ok Grandma, I am sure you had to buy clock so you could know the time," Timothy said.

"Clock? No one haffi buy clock, only if dem want. My granmada neva hab clock."

Timothy's eyes searched around from side to side. "Wait a minute," he said. "Are you saying that you lived from day to day not knowing the time?"

"Wi know de time, all wi do is look where de sun reach on de ground. Certain spot, yuh know wha time a day it is. Listen to me, when yuh walking on yuh shadow it is 12 noon. When yuh shadow is on one side a yuh it is 1 o' clock in de evening. But listen to dis. I use to hab a bed of flowers call 4 o' clock, pretty redish purplish colour. De petals open up at exactly four o' clock, it close up inna de night," Grandma Hazel explained.

"That sounds cool," Timothy said.

"How much time mi mus' tell yuh nuh use dat word?" Grandma Hazel asked. "Everyt'ing cool fi dis generation. Notin nice nor beautiful no more. Everyt'ing all yuh hear is cool, cool."

"Grandma, so at nights you do not know the time because there is no sun or flower?" Timothy asked.

"I guess they just looked through the window to see when day light," Lorna assumed.

"No," Miss Dassa answered. "Wi coulda depen pan de rooster an' de bus dem."

Timothy sighed, "Oh boy, tell me about it."

"Well de rooster crow at six every morning dat is when de cock call fi 'im draws," Miss Dassa said. "Dat is when majority a people seh dem praya an' get up. The nex' clock was de bus dem call 'May Reach'. Dat bus pass outa de cross road 4 o' clock in de morning. Only seh it neva always reliable for it bruk dung often."

"Oh, that is why they call it May Reach?" Timothy asked.

"De right name is 'May Flower'," Grandma Hazel said.

Miss Dassa continued, "Den, we did hab one nodda bus name 'Viking', dat reach roun' de deep caana 5 o' clock in de morning. Dem blow so loud when dem reach de deep caana. Dem call it 'Death Trap' caana because de worse accident dem always happen roun' dat caana. Some time is de loud bang wake up people. Nex' yuh hab was de 'Lealan' truck dat pass roun' 4 o' clock wid market people. When dat going ova de hill, all yuh hear is de vooovoo vudeen rough soun', it wake up ebry bady. Dat truck always ova load. So much people dead roun' dat caana dat de bus driva seh sometime 'im see people a stap de bus an' when 'im stap 'im coulda wait till judgement come an' look till 'im eye drop a grong, nat a smady 'im nuh see an' 'im head raise big like it gwine burse so 'im neva lef 'im red cap."

"Why he never leave his red cap?" Timothy asked.

"Den duppy nuh fraid a red," Miss Dassa replied.

"Oh yes," Lorna said. "My mom told me about a teacher whose nickname was Lealand because he used to load up several bags with food to take home from school. He was a mean teacher."

"Well," Timothy said, "There is nothing to steal from school now, not even water."

"Ebry t'ing change now," Miss Dassa said. "Inna fi wi days wi neva haffi worry bout lunch, wi ha so much food. 10 o' clock we get rich milk wid syrup in it. It smell good an' it rich so till when yuh drink it yuh pass ten chain a gas straight. An' de big chunk a real cheese from Holland. Nuh like dem sick looking cheese dem have now a days, taste lika rubba. As lilly heat ketch it, it melt turn oil, yuh haffi drink it outa de papa."

Grandma Hazel laughing, agreed with Miss Dassa. "Ha, ha, yuh rememba how lunch use to rich? Gungo peas an' rice. It rich so till yuh only need fi smell it fi get nourishment."

"Den de porridge, yuh coulda stan' up unda de sea battam an' smell it," Miss Dassa said.

"What bout de tun cornmeal wid de big chunk a pork? Dat time de cornmeal yellow. Wha dem hab now a day look like lime an' cement mix togeda. Dem days deh wi strong. Dis ya generation all dem do a sleep an' if breeze barely blow pan dem, dem either drop like nit or blow weh like feather," Grandma Hazel said.

"A true," Miss Dassa agreed.

"Last year Miss Cassy gal come spen' holiday wid her. An' every minute Miss Cassy come call mi fi look if a dead de gal dead. De gal sleep all day, all night, neva turn. Not even de cup a cold wata mi drop inna she face nuh wake her. De gal brush her face an' roll ova pan 'im gut an' dead sleep again. Mi tell poor Miss Cassey fi boil young banana gi de gal an' force her fi drink de pat wata fi strengthen her. Lawd what a change, no body nuh want fi plant notin no more," Miss Dassa concluded. She yawned, her mouth opened wide.

Grandma Hazel reached for a shoe to kill a spider that was making its way up to the ceiling, swinging from a cob web on the wall. "Yuh brute," she said as she used all the strength remaining in her aching arm to hit the innocent spider. "Come ya bwoy, tek piece a paper, pick it up an' throw it outside," she commanded Timothy.

"Up to when mi in mi 70s mi still use to plant food, now mi can't manage no more," Grandma Hazel continued.

"I remember how me an' dis laga head man use to plant food until de food talk back to we seh plant no more," Miss Dassa said, referring to her husband Maas Freddie as 'laga head' as he slept.

"Food talk back," repeated Timothy as he giggled.

"Dem ya generation lazy so till dem want yuh plant de food, cook it an' feed dem wid it," Grandma Hazel said.

Lorna disagreed. "No Grandma, I think what happen is that in those days children were not motivated to stay in school or the opportunity was not there for them to go to college and pursue careers like today. So instead of cultivating, most of us go on to educate ourselves."

CHAPTER
Five

"Misses, tan tudy, dem bwoy wha' stan' up a street side, heng out a shop paza an' sidung unda shady tree all day long wid dem big, loud music box an' big watch an' dem han', a college dem deh? A since when dem start hab college unda tree?" Miss Dassa asked.

"Nuh mussy 'Roadside University' an' 'Shady Tree College' dem deh," Grandma Hazel said.

"Inna fi mi days as a child, before we go a school, we hab ole eap a t'ings to do," Miss Dassa said. "We haffi get up before daylight, all mi hear was 'gal git up! Say yuh praya.' An' as wi say we praya, wi haffi go a bush. Sometime wi walk miles away, go feed hog, move goat an' feed rabbit. Sometimes wi haffi go a hill go look grang grang."

"Grang grang? What is that?" Timothy asked.

"Grang grang is small, dry tree limb wi use mek fire along wid de bigger dry wood," Miss Dassa answered.

"Not only dat, when wata scarce, wi haffi walk one mile or more carry wata pan wi head fi fill up de drum pan dem. Afta dat wi haffi sweep de yard wid bush, clean clean, den wi betta walk far to school an' get dere by 9 o' clock," Grandma Hazel added.

"Must be in the evening," Lorna said.

"Evening mi neck," Miss Dassa said. "I mean in de mawnin. Wi neva hab time fi sidung unda shady tree or 'Shady Tree College' or 'Roadside University'."

Miss Dassa gave Lorna a glaring look.

"Mi agree wid yuh ma, a lazy dem lazy," Miss Dassa said. "Dem fortunate, dem nuh work but dem ha big wris' watch an' dem han' a dazzle people eye. Some a dem put it on upside down. Yuh ask dem de time, dem read it backway or seh it stop work. Now a days dem hab so much time dat every six munt dem eida sen back de time or mek it run go fawud fi one hour," Miss Dassa said.

"Are you talking about daylight saving time?"Lorna asked. "They change the time in order to save energy."

"Dem brain wash oonuh so till dem soon mek oonuh believe seh a oonuh give birth to oonuh parent," Miss Dassa said. "All mi know seh is dat dem need fi leave Maasa God plan alone."

"Fi what eva reason dem doing it fa," Grandma Hazel said. "God soon come for his world."

"A true ma," Miss Dassa agreed. "God create a wonderful world give wi fi enjoy."

Lorna blew a huge bubble from the gum she was chewing. It burst, making a loud noise which frightened Miss Dassa. She made a quick twist as if to jump up from her seat. "Gal yuh frighten mi. Yuh mek mi heart almost jump tru mi mouth," she said.

"Sorry Miss Dassa," Lorna quickly apologized.

"Ha ha ha," Timothy laughed. "Mi neva know seh somebody heart can jump through dem mouth. A mussi carpenter make your heart, yuh lucky yuh alive till now Miss Dassa."

"Me an' da lille bwoy ya can neva gree. Yuh know 'im very renk, nuh have no respect fi de olda head."

"Ola head a cabbage," Timothy said laughing and running sideways. "Ola head a cabbage." Miss Dassa reached for her shoe to throw at him.

"Shut up Timothy!" Lorna shouted angrily. "Stop annoying Miss Dassa."

"Miss Dassa know seh a joke mi joking mama," Timothy replied. He stood at arms length from Miss Dassa, stretching out his arm to give her an icy mint. Miss Dassa grabbed at Timothy's hand trying to hold him, but she only caught the mint. Timothy pulled away effortlessly. Miss Dassa unwrapped the sweet and threw it in her mouth as if her mouth stood a yard from her.

Timothy laughing, said, "Mine it drop in your heart Miss Dassa."

"Nuh mine, when plantain wah dead it shoot," she said as she sucked on her icy mint, sounding as if six pigs were sucking milk from their mother all at once.

Miss Dassa was about to speak when a loud belch came out instead. "Mannas," she said. "De bwoy save mi life wid de icy mint, de gas woulda go unda mi heart an' kill mi."

Timothy loved to pick on Miss Dassa. He jumped to his feet and looked on the floor around where Miss Dassa was sitting.

"What yuh looking fah Timothy?" Grandma Hazel asked. "I hope yuh neva drop nail on de floor fi people walk on."

"No Grandma, I am looking if Miss Dassa heart jump through her mouth," Timothy answered as he giggled and kept moving sideways away from Miss Dassa.

"Go sidung! Yuh hea mi! Mi seh when plantain wa dead it shoot," she said, while pointing at Timothy.

"That's a warning Tim, you can't say Miss Dassa did not warn you," Lorna said.

CHAPTER
Six

There was a loud clap of thunder which frightened even Maas Freddie, who had been snoring like a rhinoceros. His reddened, beady eyes grew large and protruded like a fish choking on a large bait. There was a sound like small pebbles dropping on the zinc roof. They realized that it was starting to rain and thunder with lightning flashing across the sky. Everyone rushed inside as quickly as they could. The lightning dashed across the sky and mountains with sharp, bright flashes. Grandma Hazel feared lightning, so she covered the windows with sheets, since the curtains were thin. "Freddie! Freddie!" Miss Dassa shouted. "Tek out yuh false teeth, gimme mek mi put it inna mi apron pocket."

"Fi wah?" Maas Freddie asked.

"Wah yuh mean fi wah?" Miss Dassa asked. "Yuh know seh lightning draw gold an' yuh hab gold tip inna yuh teeth."

"Lawd, yuh too badaration," Maas Freddie said. "How lightning gwine ketch inna mi mouth?"

"Yuh hab de nerve a ask," Miss Dassa said. "Yuh know seh when yuh a sleep, yuh open yuh mouth like a when fowl constipated an' a pray fi deliverance."

Maas Freddie hissed his gum, his one tooth sunk into his gum making a 'tap sound' instead of a 'hiss'. Everyone laughed. Maas Freddie relaxed and closed his eyes to sleep again. Miss Dassa said, "Tro! Timothy, tek de hankechiv yah an' trow ova 'im mouth when 'im start sleep, fah me too ole fi learn sign talk."

"Sign language Miss Dassa," Timothy corrected her.

"Lorna, tek out yuh earring dem an' dem rope roun' yuh neck, an' Timothy, tek da gold something outa yuh ears. Mi nuh know a what yuh deh turn inna," Grandma Hazel said.

"Come on Grandma get modern, males can wear earrings."

Grandma Hazel started to hum a song. Although old, she maintained her angelic voice. Lorna recognized the song and joined in singing out the words. "All things bright and beautiful, all creatures great and small, all things bright and wonderful, the Lord God made them all." Timothy joined in, then Miss Dassa. They sung so loudly Maas Freddie woke up and joined them. Everyone stopped suddenly when a distinguished voice sounded like someone blowing a penny trumpet was heard. It was Maas Freddie's voice which had faded away, changing into loud snoring.

"Yes sah, sen' de rain Maasa God," Grandma Hazel said. "God work is marvelous. He told Job to stan' still an' consider His marvelous works."

"Yes mam," Miss Dassa said. "I only wish we did go home before de rain."

"Yuh can walk through the rain drops Miss Dassa," Timothy told her.

"Bwoy, a tell yuh wa tell mi seh mi maga like lead pencil? When mi did young mi did hab little flesh pan mi body," Miss Dassa said.

"So, is what you have now mam, clay?" Timothy asked.

"Bwoy tan tuddy mek Maasa God rain fall," Miss Dassa said.

"The rain did not stop when I started to talk," Timothy said.

"Shut up bwoy," Grandma Hazel commanded him. She started to hum again. "When de thunders roll, God is thundering marvelously with His voice."

"Are you saying God's voice sounds like thunder Grandma?" Lorna asked.

"A God voice yes, ehe, ehe, yuh nuh hear nothing yet, de trumpet louder dan Him voice. The small shower or de big shower of rain is God strength."

"That would look more like tears to me," Lorna said.

"Well," said Grandma Hazel, "If a eye wata any at all, is cry God crying ova how people change His wonderful world dat He create, but de bible neva seh eye wata, it seh strength. All dem people in America crying bout snow, is God command de snow to come on de earth. Charmaine seh some part a America is only frost, no snow. De frost is God breath. De bible seh God sen' snow out of de north."

"A true," Lorna said. "That is why it snows up north so much."

"Firs' time people use to seh when rain falling, is cry God crying, but God neva have notin much fi cry ova dem time deh. So much wickedness neva a gwaan," Miss Dassa said.

"A true ma," Grandma Hazel agreed. "Now 'im mussi a bawl fi true fi si what 'im beautiful world that 'im create gone to. In fi wi days, when yuh do hear bout some mad smaddy kill anada one, is machete dem use chop dem up or poison dem mostly if somebody t'ief. Now a days is gun dem shoot. Inna fi wi days de only time yuh hear gun shot is when Busha or de nex' Backra man what did live up ova de hill tap a shoot white belly bird out a 'im corn field an' 'im pimento tree. A mad de busha man mad why 'im use gun shoot de bird."

"Why he neva use catapult?" Timothy asked.

"Maybe he does not know how to use catapult," Lorna replied.

"Probably," Grandma Hazel said. "Yuh did know seh all de wirlwind yuh see, it come from de south?"

"Is that in the bible also?" Lorna asked.

"Yes, read Proverb 37, it tell yuh every t'ing what I jus' tell yuh."

"When rain fall de thick cloud get tiad an' worn out so den God scatter de bright cloud all ova de sky," Grandma Hazel said.

"Oh," Lorna said. "After a dark cloud comes silver clouds. Oh, I see, yuh right Grandma."

"What yuh seh? She right yes, she nuh ask yuh if she right. Mama Hay Hay read her bible, she know wha she deh seh," Miss Dassa replied.

"Eh mi dear ma," Grandma Hazel said, smiling and rocking slowly back and forth. "Look how long mi use to preach, is only now since mi get sickly an' ole I stop, but mi still know mi bible."

Timothy laughing, said, "Dem ya generation ya only know fi read love book."

"Shut up Timothy," Lorna said, throwing her slipper at him.

The slipper hit Maas Freddie on his ear instead. He jumped. "A wha? Ooh ooh," he said as he grabbed his ear. Then he was fast asleep again.

"Watch 'im," Miss Dassa said in disgust. "Good fi 'im, 'im snore too much."

"Lorna be careful, suppose yuh did lick off de man ears or injury 'im ears mek 'im deaf," Grandma Hazel said.

"It would neva mek a deference for 'im hab de two big ears an' 'im deaf like a fish, might as well 'im neva have none," Miss Dassa said.

"Poor t'ing, me caa hear a t'ing sometime neida," Grandma Hazel said.

"A lazy Freddie ears lazy, jus like de res a 'im body," Miss Dassa said.

"Miss Dassa, fish nuh deaf, is bat deaf," Timothy told her.

"A weh yuh get dat from?" she asked. "All a dem deaf, fish, bat an' Freddie."

"And Grandma," Timothy added.

"An' yuh pa," replied Grandma Hazel.

"No Grandma, Amiah is not deaf," Lorna intervened.

"'Im deaf yes," Grandma said. "If 'im neva deaf 'im would hear when mi tell 'im to leave yuh alone when 'im jus start court yuh, instead 'im stick on pon yuh like sticking plasta till 'im give yuh Timoty, den suddenly de sticking plasta stick no more."

"'Im t'ink yuh said neva leave her nor forsake her, eva be her friend until a baby comes," said Timothy.

"Keep your lips closed together," Lorna told him.

"Yes Mom, not like Maas Freddie," Timothy said.

Everyone was looking at Maas Freddie, his lips were hanging open contentedly.

"Grandma, please continue telling us about God's power and do not pay Timothy any mind," Lorna told her.

"Yes, as mi was saying. When God sen' rain, is either fi correction, to wata 'im land or fi mercy."

"Mercy?" Timothy asked. "Miss Mercy?"

"No idiot," Lorna answered. "Mercy, meaning grace, or compassion or blessing."

"Dats right," Grandma Hazel said.

"Ebry bady know seh Timothy nuh ha no sense," Miss Dassa said.

"I have sense enough to know that my heart can't jump through my mouth Miss Dassa."

"Grandma is waiting to continue her teaching," Lorna said.

Everyone was quiet except for the heavy drops of rain on the zinc and window panes. "God control everyt'ing in dis world, even de animals, fish, bird, reptile and trees. That is why all species are different," Lorna said.

"Yuh right mi child, some 'im mek wise an' some foolish," Grandma Hazel said. "Yuh did know dat God keep de snow in a store room? 'Im said 'Im keep dem ready fi times of trouble an' days of battle an' war."

"Where in the bible you saw that Grandma?" Timothy asked.

"Go an' get yuh bible boy, an' look for Job chapter 38 v. 22 when God ask Job if 'im eva visit de store room where 'im keep de snow an' hail."

Timothy dropped the knife and the piece of cane he was eating and ran to fetch his bible. He read the verse. "A true," he said, showing it to Lorna.

"So," replied Lorna. "Grandma knows what she is saying."

"Nuh fawud de bwoy fawud," Miss Dassa said. She cut her eyes at Timothy and instructed him to have a seat.

Grandma Hazel continued, "Yes, as mi was saying, even when de Lord command de lightning to flash, de lightning go to de Lord an' seh at your service. Better dan dat; dere is a bird inna ancient Egypt name 'Tbis'. De Lord tell de bird when de river will flood, so whenever de bird come roun' an' chirp, de River Nile flood. Even de rooster dem know when rain ago fall."

"How do the roosters know Grandma?" Lorna asked.

"No de Lord tell dem," she replied.

"What is their reaction when rain is going to fall?" Lorna asked.

"Not sure," replied Grandma Hazel. "Either dem crow an' look up in de sky or maybe when yuh see two rooster ah talk."

"No," Miss Dassa said. "When two rooster talking, dem seh a visita yuh going to hab so, a mussi when dem look up in de sky an' crow fi de rain come from up dere."

"How comes I never see them talking, neither looking up nor crowing when you and Maas Freddie was coming this evening?" Timothy asked, not because he believed but he wanted to be sarcastic. "I am going to start watching the roosters."

"The Lord count de cloud dem an' tilt dem ova to pour out de rain," Grandma Hazel said.

"Oh, so when the rain falls the Lord tilts the clouds, meaning that the rain is under the clouds," Timothy verified.

"No, de Lord tilt de cloud an' mek de rain fall, yes de rain is unda de cloud," Grandma Hazel replied. "All dem bird yuh shoot yuh know seh when de young raven cry, is de Lord dem crying to for food, jus' like how we pray fi weh we need."

"Raven?" Timothy asked. "Dem craven, must be how dem get dem name, me not shooting anymore."

"Well, even de ostrich. God mek dem wing beat fas' but yet God seh no ostrich can fly like stork."

"A true," Timothy said. "The ostrich's wings beat fast fast but the long legged stork flies faster."

"Tap seh a true bwoy like yuh t'ink a lie yuh granma deh tell. Oonuh generation t'ink oonuh know it all," Miss Dassa said.

"But listen to dis," said Gandma Hazel. "God mek de ostrich foolish, 'im neva give dem any wisdom. The Lord seh when de ostrich start run she can laugh afta any horse an' de rida. Dat mean de ostrich can run fasa dan a horse an' rida."

"A true," Timothy said. "Oh, a mean dats right, no I mean, I see, ostrich run faster than a horse."

Miss Dassa looked at Timothy with crossed eyes. "Bwoy yuh anaying like maskitta an' yuh ears tough lika fi hog."

"I neva said a word mam," Timothy turning his back to Miss Dassa.

"An' yuh renk like a ram goat," Miss Dassa added, cutting her eyes. Her mouth opened wide, exposing her two teeth standing alone on either side of her mouth. One upstairs looking down and one downstairs looking up.

Lorna cleared her throat. "Grandma, you said God did not give wisdom to the ostrich, he made her foolish. How does one know she is foolish?"

"Well," Grandma Hazel explained, "de ostrich lef' har eggs inna de groun' fi de heat in de groun' to keep dem warm, instead of har sitting on dem an' warm dem. She nuh sit on dem like de fowl. She nuh even t'ink seh foot will walk on dem an' mash dem up. She act like de egg dem not even belong to har, she not even care seh she wase har effort."

"Yes, a true," Timothy said, standing up and getting excited. Timothy quickly covered his mouth and looked at Miss Dassa. "Sorry," he said. "I mean I see ostrich eggs unda the ground all de time. Grandma is that found in Job 38 too?"

"No, it inna chapter 39, look at verse 14 to 18."

Timothy read it aloud.

"Oh bwoy, I must read my bible more, this is interesting, there is a lot to learn," Lorna said.

Miss Dassa looked at Lorna and asked her, "Yuh going to read bible? Dat a musa when all de TV dem grow foot an' start run bout. Yuh gwine start read bible?"

"We jus' haffi pray fi dem mi dear ma. What nuh happen in a year, happen in a day," Grandma Hazel said.

Miss Dassa tried to get up. "Dem ya generation ya," she said as she brushed a peenie wallie from her skirt. "If yuh ask dem what de name a de firs' chapter in de bible dem nuh know. Dem only know what time ebry show come on pan TV."

"Genesis!" Timothy shouted. "Seet deh Miss Dassa, I know my bible." Timothy, challenging Miss Dassa, asked, "I bet you can't tell me how many books in the bible?"

"Book inna bible? Book caa inna bible, yuh mean how much leaf in de bible? How mi fi know dat bwoy? De bible is one book, some a dem big, some little."

"There are sixty-six books in the bible Miss Dassa," Lorna told her.

"How sixty-six book fi hold inna one book? Oonuh t'ink mi a idiot?"

There was a burst of laughter. "Hay Hay, you know de bible," Miss Dassa said. "Sixty-six book caa inna one bible, yuh eva hear any t'ing like dat?"

"Yes mam, remember it start wid Genesis an' end with Revelation."

"Oh, a dat dem a talk bout, a sixty-six a dem. Oonuh know more dan mi, sometime mi head mix up."

"Boo boo boo," Timothy said, making funny faces at Miss Dassa.

"Bwoy girout, yuh hear seh me an' yuh a no size."

Timothy stood at arms length beside Miss Dassa, measuring up to her. "I am taller than you, that's why me and yuh a nuh size," Timothy said, running away as he spoke.

"Nuh run," Miss Dassa said as she laughed, exposing the two watchmen sitting in her mouth. "Mi bed a call mi now." She yawned loudly.

"Lawd Miss Dassa, yuh nearly swallow all of us the way you opened your mouth wide," Timothy told her.

"Go weh bwoy, mi couldn't swalla yuh, yuh a pure skellingtan, yuh woulda choke mi."

"Miss Dassa, read my lips, say skeleton," Timothy said.

Everyone laughed except Maas Freddie. Miss Dassa looked at him. He was fast asleep. His mouth was open and he was drooling. His scrawny neck hung to one side.

Miss Dassa shook him by his shoulder. "Wake up Freddie! Mi bed a call mi," she said. Maas Freddie tried to get up. His beady eyes rolled in their orbits.

"Dassa, day light a ready?" he asked, falling back in the chair. His flacid body wobbled like jello as he tried to get up again.

"Lawd, yuh always fall asleep ebry weh yuh go an' wake up a chat foolishness. Come wi go home. Yuh so fool fool when yuh a sleep."

"Mi hear yuh seh get up, mi figat seh mi no deh home an' fall a sleep."

"Ebry weh yuh go yuh fall asleep. Yuh mussi ha dropsy."

Maas Freddie was fast asleep again. "Freddie! Wake up!" She shook him vigorously by his shoulder. "Dats why mi nuh like go no weh wid yuh, yuh always act like tiad donkey, yuh only need yuh tail. Git up, yuh bahine no ha no manners."

"Coffee give gas," Grandma Hazel said.

"Coffee or no coffee, Freddie bahine always outa control," Miss Dassa replied.

"Poor t'ing," Grandma Hazel said.

"Giddy up!" said Timothy, laughing.

"Go tell yuh play mate giddy up bwoy, mi look like a donkey to yuh?" Maas Freddie asked.

"Yuh act like one," Miss Dassa answered.

"Mi enjoy de company," Grandma Hazel said.

"Please come again," Lorna added.

Grandma Hazel had already poured more kerosene oil in the bottle torch and made a new cork out of brown paper. She tilted the bottle to soak the cork in the oil, then lit it, making a bright torch. The rain had stopped and the fresh smell of dew on the green grass refreshed the air. Frogs croaked and crickets whistled loudly. There was a patoo sitting comfortably under the window sill asking "A hoo? A hoo?", his eyes shining brightly. Grandma Hazel looked at the weird creature and said, "Yuh inquisitive wretch yuh, stay deh asking a hoo, a hoo. None a yuh business."

Lorna was afraid that the couple would accidentally light their heads a fire with the torch. She took her flash light and asked Timothy to put out the torch. "I will walk with you," Lorna said.

"No!" Grandma Hazel said. "Timothy can go. Too much bwoy bout de place an' some a dem love eben up dem self pan people decent gal pickney. Den if a de bottle lamp yuh carry, yuh could light dem blinkin head a fiah. But no, yuh too stush fi carry bottle lamp."

"Grandma, men do not only rape girls, they rape boys too," Lorna told her.

Grandma Hazel was quiet for a while, her eyes wondered with her mind. "What a life," she said.

"Inna fi wi days, only females yuh hear seh dem rape. Now dem start fi rape every t'ing," Maas Freddie said.

"Mi dear sah," Grandma Hazel said.

"Dem will rape you too Maas Freddie," Timothy told him.

"Mi?" Maas Freddie asked, rolling his beady eyes. "Mi too ole, mi woulda kick de bucket before dem coulda even tek off mi clothes."

"Nobody would spend time taking off your clothes Maas Freddie. They would cut it off," Timothy said. "And cut you too."

"What a change," he said.

"It's time you stop using bottle lamp Grandma and start using flashlight. It is civilized time now," Lorna told her as she walked away.

"Oonuh an' oonuh civilization gwine turn oonuh inna parpurization, dis gimme mi bottle torch an' gallang weh oonuh going. Nuh mek mi see one peenie fly pass mi before oonuh come back."

"I am grown Grandma," Lorna replied. "I can take care of myself."

"Grown fool," Grandma muttered under her breath. "All bout a oonuh kin outa door fi mek man a touch up touch up oonuh kin, bout yuh grown. Timoty! Timoty! A sleep yuh drap a sleep aready bwoy? Gittup! Come walk wid da hard ears gal go down a road an' come back."

Grandma Hazel stood at the door holding the bottle torch in her hand until they disappeared in the dark shadows of the night.

CHAPTER
Seven

Grandma Hazel glanced at the beautiful yellow flowers that were unfolding their petals, while the pretty multicoloured butterflies danced around. "A four o' clock aready! De four o' clock flowers start opening out," she said.

Grandma Hazel had just finished washing the clothes and was hanging them on the wire clothes line. She sold snacks to the children in the neighbourhood. Surprised at the time, she said, "De school children dem soon come to buy ncaseberry an' suck-suck an' mi nat even tek out de neaseberry dem yet."

She hurried to fetch the basin of ripe neaseberries, setting it on the edge of the verandah. She then sat in her old wooden rocking chair. "A how Timoty nuh come back fram de library yet? " she wondered aloud.

The loud voices of the school children could be heard in the distance. "Yuh little retch yuh! If yuh eva trow one more rockstone in dat neaseberry tree!" she shouted, as a little boy tried to use a stone to hit a neaseberry from the tree. He was terrified and ran as fast as he could.

Just then, a group of children stopped to buy neaseberries and suck-suck. "Grandma Hazel! Grandma Hazel!" a little girl shouted while she ran breathlessly up the steep hill. "Timoty seh to tell yuh 'im stop at de pos' office, but de line long mam. 'Im soon come home mam."

"T'anks mi dalin," she replied. She handed a neaseberry to the little girl. She grabbed it fast, and bit into it without mercy while running through the gate. "Come back here!" Grandma Hazel shouted. She took the neaseberry from her. "What yuh sopose to say when somebody give yuh somet'ing?" she asked.

The little girl nervously replied, "T'anks mam." She took the neaseberry and continued biting into it.

"Mi nuh kno' what happen to dese children nowadays, dem nuh have no mannas. I could neva t'ink of taking t'ings out a people han' an' not even seh t'anks. De pickney nearly drag mi han' outa socket," she said.

Timothy shouted from the gate, "Grandma! Mama write you."

"Bwoy yuh frighten mi," she replied. Her face glowed with happiness.

"It feels like money in there," Timothy said, pressing on the envelope.

"Dats all you care bout, money," she said as she snatched the envelope from Timothy's hand.

"Merciful fadah!" she exclaimed, her face masked with surprise. "My God! An' all dis time mi neva kno'." She hurriedly refolded the letter.

"What happen Grandma?" Timothy inquired.

"Yuh mada in de fambly way," she replied.

"What does that mean Grandma?" he asked.

"It mean you going to get either a brada or sista," she replied.

"Ha, haah," Timothy laughed, "me know long time."

"Wait, Lorna tell you an' neva tell me?"

"No Grandma, mama didn't tell me anything, but I could tell because her belly did start getting big and she kept spitting and eating the green, sour gimbilin night and day."

"I coulda neva tell, an' she due next month," Grandma Hazel said.

Grandma Hazel was quiet for a while. She seemed lost. She sat with her hands on her cheeks and her elbows piercing her thighs. "Well de horse gone trough de gate aready, mek no sense cry ova spilt milk," she said. "I betta start packing my grip from now to go a town. I don't know how mi going to manage because mi neva go a town before."

"Do not worry Grandma, remember I can go with you," Timothy reassured her.

"How in de name of God yuh can go wid mi, so who will take care of de fowl an' rabbit dem?"she asked. "Yuh can stay wid parson an' his wife an' come up every day come look afta de fowl an' de rabbit dem, an' mek sure yuh go back down. You hab some tough ears but you betta do exactly as I seh." Though Grandma Hazel spoke sternly, Timothy insisted on going to Kingston with her. He had alternatives.

"Grandma, we could ask Rupert to take care of them," he said.

"Who, yuh mad bwoy?" Grandma Hazel asked angrily. "Rupert who walk an' tief people fowl an' cook dem wid de fedda an de gut an' eat dem like hawk. Why yuh t'ink dem call 'im hawk? Even when de fowl dem lay egg, 'im nuh wait till de egg cool, 'im suck dem out raw like mangoose."

"Oh, Miss Dasssa and Maas Freddie could take care of them Grandma."

"Bwoy yuh start use dat ganja bush agen? Yuh mad? Yuh nuh si Maas Freddie 'im walk like when fowl a carry corn bush an' Miss Dassa, dat poor t'ing can scarcely stand up. De only person I would ask is dat bwoy dem call Rawmeat."

"Ha, ha, ha, haah," Timothy laughed. "His name is Raymet, not rawmeat, I would not trust him with the rabbits and fowl."

"So how you trust Hawk?" Grandma Hazel asked. "I will ask de bwoy."

"Raymet Grandma, Raymet," Timothy reminded her.

Grandma Hazel stood on the verandah looking around as if confused. "My God, I don't know where fi start. De ole grip musbe full a dus'. Is years now it nuh use," she said.

"But Grandma, nobody don't use grip no more. Remember Grandma, Charmaine left two big suitcase filled with things, you could use them," Timothy reminded her.

Grandma Hazel became furious. "What yuh mean nobady nuh use grip no more? Well, is my grip an' de 'two side basket' me carrying, an' mek mi si a who going to stap mi fram carrying dem. You go eat your dinna an' wash up de plate dem. Mi going to my bed early an' get up early. Mi haffi get some tea bush an' bath bush fi Lorna. Some to use mek bath fi her nine days afa she hab her baby, an' some to mek tea fi she drink fi clean her out, for sometime all de 'afta birt' nuh come out an' it will mek her sick." Grandma Hazel had very little or no idea as to the changes that have taken place over the years, and it was impossible for Timothy to convince her.

"Grandma, you just going to waste your time. Don't bother with any bush, mama not going to use them. People don't do those things anymore. They have many different antibiotics to treat infection. There are all sorts of nice therapeutic baths and nice smelling bubble baths now. People don't just pick bush and boil baths anymore Grandma, that is what will make them sick," Timothy said.

"Bwoy shet yuh mouth. Yuh a young bird, yuh nuh kno' hurricane."

"What does that mean Grandma? I have seen hurricane before."

"It mean yuh young. Yuh nuh hab nuh experience in dese t'ings," Grandma Hazel explained. "All dem foolish bath yuh talking bout, a de same bush dem use, dem only process it an' full it up wid chemical an' cush-cush wata what dem call fragants."

"Fragrance Grandma," Timothy interrupted.

"Hab mannas bwoy! Nuh cut mi off," she shouted. "Dat is why ounuh sick so. Yuh eva si mi sick bwoy? Yuh eva si mi go inna hospital go lie dung like mi nuh hab no sense? Go sidung one side an' shet yuh fool fool mout; bout bath mek people sick." Grandma Hazel hissed her teeth and walked away. She fell asleep on her knees, while praying for her granddaughter. She was awakened by the loud noise of a young coconut that fell on the zinc roof. She passed the night thinking about Lorna and dozing off in short bouts of slumber.

CHAPTER
Eight

Grandma Hazel heard the rooster crowing and quickly got out of bed. She was so much accustomed to use the crowing of the rooster as her clock, that she was able to hear them even in her deepest sleep. "A six o' clock aready! I wanda if I neva hear de second cock crow." She listened for a while. "Wait a minute, but nuh busha noisy truck dat, a six o' clock yes." She knelt to pray. The roosters were crowing loudly and flapping their wings. The loud horn from the May Flower bus could be heard miles away. The fowls were flying off their roost. The birds were whistling happy tunes and calling each other. The nightingale sung its last solo and flew away into the woods. The loud croaking of frogs and whistling of toads, all together welcomed the new day.

Grandma Hazel stood at the window looking at the coming dawn. A gush of cool fresh air rushed in as she opened the jalousie windows. The sweet scent of the roses and the blue forget-me-nots perfumed the air.

Grandma Hazel shouted, "Timoty! Come here!"

"Mi feeding de fowl dem Grandma," Timothy replied. He was helping himself with some ripe sweet neaseberries.

"Before mi figet, mi wa yuh fi go dung a Doc drugs store an' buy some horsifetita fi put pon de baby mole so it nuh catch up cole before de mole close," she told Timothy. Timothy mumbled quietly, "Not again."

Grandma Hazel was so used to Timothy's grumbling she assumed he would have made a smart comment. She angrily asked, "What yuh a grumble seh bwoy?"

"Mama not even going to use dem," he said.

"Look if de sun reach unda de top step yet, dat mean it would be nine o' clock. Dose fowl lay dem eggs exactly nine o' clock every morning. Yuh haffi pick dem up before de confounded mangoose get dem."

"Grandma, how come you do not look at the clock when you need to know the time?" Timothy asked.

"Mi neva baan come see my parents dem wid clock, is de sun dem use to know de time in de day an in de night wi listen when de rooster crow. De rooster crow tree times same exact time every time. Rememba, in de bible, Jesus did tell Peter, he will deny 'im Jesus when de cock crow trice. He did nat seh how much o' clock. Some times we can tell de time when de bus an' market truck dem blow roun' de corna, but dem not reliable because some times dem break dung a road. Clock wrong sometime. Maasa God sun neva wrong an' de rooster neva wrong. I tell yuh all de time, nature comes wid God power. God give man knowledge to mek t'ings, but dem nuh hab God power."

CHAPTER
Nine

"Timoty! Timotee!" Grandma Hazel shouted. "Where dat bwoy dissappear to?"

"Yes Grandma! Coming Grandma," he answered from a distance. Timothy came back with some star apples. "I pick these for mama, she loves star apples."

"Later in de evening or yuh betta go now, mi wah yuh fi go an' sen' a telegram to Lorna fi expec' wi on de 'May Flower' bus on Tursday."

"Thursday?" Timothy asked. "It betta we go on Wednesday, Grandma. Too much market people take the bus on Thursdays and you can't stand all the way to Kingston."

Grandma Hazel, well known for her stubborn ways, became angry. Ignoring Timothy's advice, she sternly shouted, "Do as mi seh! De bus caa full before it reach Cross Road."

Timothy was used to his great-grandmother's ways and had very little fear of her anger. He loved and respected her very much but would from time to time behave as a normal teenager.

"Gandma, you don't need to send telegram. I will go to Donovan's house and send an e-mail."

"Seh what bwoy?" Grandma Hazel asked.

"E-mail," Timothy repeated.

Grandma Hazel had not the slightest idea what Timothy was talking about. "How in de name of God mail fi reach town by Tursday an' she need fi get it by Wednesday de lates'?" she asked, her face creased with concern.

"She will get an e-mail in a second Grandma, telegram is no longer necessary." Timothy, patting Grandma Hazel on her shoulder, said, "Get into the world of modern technology Grandma."

"Siah bwoy, yuh do exactly as mi tell yuh. Mi nuh know what you call v-mail or t-mail. Mi not into oonuh foolishness. Now what in de wirl going to reach town eighty miles away in de space a one secon'?" she asked. "Yuh need fi stay wid yuh ma when you go up a town for a nuh notin but de stinkin' bush yuh go smoke every chance yuh get."

Timothy walked close up to his Grandma, opened his mouth and breathed on her nose. "Smell my breath Grandma, what I told you is real. You just don't understand Grandma."

Timothy's breath seemed to need attention. Grandma Hazel took a step backwards and shouted, "Bwoy! My God! A rotten fish yuh jus' done eat? Go wash yuh mout' wid vinegar an' wata."

Timothy tried to explain. "Alright Grandma, when we go to Kingston I am going to show you mom's computer. It works like a miracle, Grandma. It is called Internet. You can talk to people all over the world and do transactions in seconds. It connects the whole world."

Grandma Hazel paused for a while, listening, but stubbornly pretended as if she was totally ignoring Timothy. She placed her hands on her hips and said, "Any bady eva hear mi calamity? Dem seh de Antichris would act like he is God, so now yuh seh it work miracle so it mus be de Antichris machine. Git up! Go wash de star apple stain off yuh mout an' go sen de telegram."

Timothy walked away as fast as he could, fearing she would throw something at him. "Is e-mail me sending Grandma, you don't understand," Timothy concluded.

"So help mi God, if yuh nuh do as I seh, yuh stay wid yuh ma when yuh go upa town, yuh not ruling me, a me birth yuh muma, an' yuh muma birth you, ano you birth me," Grandma Hazel said in a rather outrageous manner.

Miss Dassa stopped by. She sat on a rock under a shade tree to catch her breath and cool off, fanning her face with a cocoa leaf. "Lawd Hay Hay de heat a kill mi. Mi haffi res' unda de cool Ma," she said. She came just in time to enjoy a cool drink of lemonade made from wet cane sugar with sour orange and chipped ice. The cup was made from dried, cured shell which was known to keep liquids cool. Miss Dassa looked at Grandma Hazel and said, "Yuh face no look so plesant Hay Hay, yuh musa tiad."

"Mi tiad yes, but is nat so much of de tiredness ma. Dis a more dan tiadness." Grandma Hazel took a seat beside her friend. "Mi dear Miss Dassa, mi caa stay wid yuh because mi packing fi go to town tomorrow mawnin."

"Town!" Miss Dassa exclaimed. Her mouth drooped open like a hungry bird.

"Shhhh," Grandma Hazel said. "Nuh bada go tell Tom, Dick an' Harry, keep it quiet." Grandma Hazel was afraid her house would be burglarized while she was away.

"A wha happen Hay Hay?" Miss Dassa asked.

"Lawd mi dear ma, trouble nuh set like rain. Nuh Lorna in de fambily way," replied Grandma Hazel.

"Ooоo," said Miss Dassa.

"An' she nuh married," Grandma Hazel said. "Is a burden shame."

"A shame yes ma," Miss Dassa agreed.

"Den, a next week she due yuh kno'."

"Seh wha! Mercy, mercy an' all dis time she a hide it fram yuh. A only hope de yung man gwine marry her! A oh!" said Miss Dassa, jerking her shoulders and pursing her lips tight.

"A Friday mi get de telegram seh she due next munt. Neva even kno' she impregnated, so I tell Timoty to go sen' a telegram fi tell her we coming Tuesday. Mi dear Ma, de bwoy nuh come tell mi seh him going to 'im fren yawd go sen some kina mail or anada, v-mail, t-mail some nonsense like dat, bout she wi get it quicka dan de telegram. Yuh eva hear such foolishness mi dear ma?" Grandma Hazel asked.

Miss Dassa had been a bit more alert of changes and was also a little more in the modern world than her friend Grandma Hazel. "Oh, ano dat Hay Hay. De bwoy nuh say it right. A 'in de net' dem call it. Dem seh is a whole wirl machine. De whole wirl inna it ma. School, church, bank, shop, store, hospital. Ebry t'ing what deh pan God earth ma," replied Miss Dassa.

"Me nuh t'ink yuh hear good ma," Grandma Hazel said.

Miss Dassa gave Grandma Hazel a glaring look. "Me nuh hear good, mi hear good good ma, de only ting nuh inna dat net a musa heaven, but hell in deh ma. Mi neva seet yet, but mi hear de young people dem talk bout it. Even Maas Busha have one. A him firs' eena de district buy one."

"I wanda if a dat mi hear meking noise ova Mass Busha yawd, soun' like when truck going ova steep hill?" Grandma Hazel wondered.

"No ma, is de delco plant yuh hear. Mi hear Chiquita big mout' gal was a cus off Busha shaggy head bwoy las' week. She tell him no bady nuh want him a dat why 'im haffi go inna de net go look woman. So it look like de mallatta gal what him hab, a outa de net she come from," Miss Dassa said.

"Siah God, den yuh mean even people live inna it?" Grandma Hazel asked.

"Yuh nuh hear notin yet, mi hear seh people even do rudeness in deh, for mi hear Busha bwoy tell de gal seh 'im nuh want her, before 'im hab any t'ing fi do wid her 'im go pan de net."

"Mi dear Miss Dassa, if mi neva kno' seh you nuh smoke, mi would t'ink you deh smoke de bush like Timoty. All mi can seh, like I said before, a nuh notin but de Antichris dea try fi fool people," Grandma Hazel said. "De bible seh many will be fooled. Den wait a minute, if Timoty gone sen' message to Lorna in de net, den a wanda if Lorna in dere to?"

"Me caa tell yuh much bout it ma, it soun' funny to me," replied Miss Dassa.

"What a hell of a machine dat net musbe," Grandma Hazel said. "So, dem soon stamp de '666' on wi forehead an' give wi de card fi buy what dem allow wi fi buy," she added.

"Yes, yes my God, my God," Miss Dassa said, covering her mouth with her hand as if burnt by hot corn meal. "Jesus Saviour of de wirl! Hay Hay, yuh right. Mi hear Maas Busha daughta seh she use her card buy t'ings in de net, wow, wow, wow."

"Well, de only people dat will hurt is de lazy one dem who don't plant anyt'ing," Grandma Hazel said.

"A true ma," Miss Dassa agreed. "Mi run eena Missa Brown boasy bwoy outa de shop. Mi ask de lazy bwoy how come 'im mek 'im fadah lan' jus' stay an' wase like dat since 'im dead, if 'im caa plant somet'ing. Hear what de bwoy seh, 'Mi Ma? De only time fi mi han' dem touch de grung is when something drop from me'. Mi jus' cut mi eye afta 'im an walk wey for if 'im pa han' neva touch dirt 'im coulda neva dead an' lef' so much lan' an' money fi 'im. Mi hear seh a nuff money so till even one a de Prime Minista dem, mi nuh kno' which one, did a try fi borrow money fram 'im unda de quiat. A Busha let de puss outa de bag. Any where yuh si dat bwoy, 'im always hab 'im han' inna 'im pocket. I wanda how 'im manage when 'im use de toilet if 'im hia somebody fi help 'im? Mek 'im stay deh ma, mi hear seh every t'ing wi hab, even plantation, a de antichrist going to control it," Miss Dassa said.

"Well, mek mi si a which antichris or unclechris going to control what mi hab. If a so, God will destroy dat net," Grandma Hazel said as she got up and slapped the arthritis out of her hips. "Listen Miss Dassa, mi begging yuh an' Maas Freddie to give a eye on de yawd till mi come back. Rawmeat will take care of de fowl an' de rabbit dem."

"Raw wha Hay Hay?" Miss Dassa asked. "Yuh mean Rawmat?"

Timothy came back. "Raymet, Miss Dassa. You always never say things right," he said. "Grandma, I send the e-mail to mama and she answer back and said she is glad we are coming but you must not load up your self with anything when you are coming."

Miss Dassa had always been a contradictory person who seemed to hear things close to the facts. She interrupted the conversation. "Hush yuh mout' bwoy, notin nuh name 'eh-mail' a 'in-de-net' it name, bout mi neva seh t'ings right. A young bwoy like yuh mek a ole woman like mi know de name betta dan you."

"Look Miss Dassa, read my lips, in-ter-net, not in- de - net," Timothy emphasized. "I sent the e-mail by way of the Internet."

"What de difference?" Miss Dassa asked, shooting sprinkles of spit in the air. Grandma Hazel looked at the paper. "Timoty, mi tell yuh fi sen' a telegram. Den, who fah name yuh sign at de bottom?" Grandma Hazel asked.

"Nobody, Grandma," he replied.

"So how in de name a God she will kno' who it coming fram?" she asked.

"It's ok Gandma," Timothy reassured her.

"Mi nuh want mi name in dat antichris machine!" she shouted.

"It is not antichris machine Grandma. It is a wonderful invention. Don't listen to Miss Dassa," Timothy advised her.

"Girout bwoy," Miss Dassa said, throwing her hands up in the air as if trying to fly. "Hay, Hay mi gwine miss yuh, mek hase come back. De Lord go with yuh an' be careful ma, we living inna serious time."

"A true mi dear Ma," replied Grandma Hazel. "Mi going to miss you, but tek good care of yuh self an' Maas Freddie." They hugged each other.

Timothy loved Miss Dassa and Maas Freddie. He respected them very much and enjoyed picking on them all the time. Timothy, laughing, asked, "So, Miss Dassa, when the Lord go with us, who stay with you?"

"God is ebry where mi bwoy," she replied, "ebry where. Yuh try nuh get in any trouble mi bwoy, even dough yuh badda mi so."

"You know I love you Miss Dassa," Timothy reassured her.

Grandma Hazel had been preparing for her trip all week.

"Timoty, yuh carry de grip. I will carry de basket. Oh, yuh haffi carry de box too," she said.

"Grandma me not carrying that old grip, people will be looking at me. I will use one of Aunt Charmaine luggage," Timothy replied, as he rudely walked away and took a seat on the step.

"Charmaine what bwoy?" Grandma Hazel asked. She was displaying the most disgusted look on her face. "Mi nuh kno' wah yuh call lug an' edge, but all mi kno' Charmaine carry her t'ings fram ova seas an' yuh nat putting yuh han' on notin fi her," she warned Timothy sternly.

He walked off hastily through the gate. "I'm going to e-mail Aunt Charmaine and ask her if I can use it."

"I cah tek de badaration wid no granpickney. Now 'im tek up habit wid dat devil machine Miss Dassa seh name 'in-de-net'. So, it seem like once yuh get caught inna it, yuh haffi keep going an' neva stop. A lef' him right here tomorrow mawnin," she said.

Timothy came running through the gate with a sheet of paper in his hand. "Grandma, Aunt Charmaine send you a e-mail. I print it out for you, read it Grandma," he said.

"Bwoy, get outta mi way wid dat destruction paper you an' de devil write!" Grandma Hazel shouted. Every vein in her neck was fully engorged.

"Grandma, please, please read it," Timothy pleaded. "Ok, I will read it to you Grandma."

Pointing her stick at Timothy, she said, "Get outa mi way bwoy before I get mi self in trouble. How in de name of God Charmaine fi sen' letta here, all de way from America in de space of twenty minute?" she asked.

"One second Grandma," Timothy replied.

"Not even telegram coulda come so fas'. I tell Lorna seh yuh still smoke de ganja bush, but she nuh believe mi. My God, mi sorry, but mi nuh want no more gran nor great gran nor no sorta gran pickney here fi grieve my soul, an' si, she gone hab pickney again."

Timothy insisted on reading the message. He stood afar from his grandmother, reading it out loudly, "Mother dear, I am delighted to know that you finally decided to take a trip to Kingston, and that you will be there for my daughter during her most difficult time. Feeling so bad I am unable to be there due to my demanding job. Timothy can use the luggage, you should use it also. I think the grip is a bit too old fashioned. I hope your next trip will be to America. Have a safe trip. Enjoy your time mother. I love you dearly, kisses."

Grandma stood looking amazed at Timothy. "Stanup right dere, nuh move." She repeated the twenty third psalm, then snatched the paper from Timothy. "De gates of hell cannot prevail against God's people." She then read the message. Grandma Hazel glanced at Timothy with a disturbed look. "Afta anuh Charmaine write dis, an' where she sign it?" she asked.

"Listen Grandma," Timothy said, walking closer up to her. "She typed it on the computer, then she e-mailed me and then I printed it from the computer."

"Nuh complicate mi ole brain," she said, handing the paper to Timothy. "Firs' a did 't-mail' den 'in-de-net', now a 'computya'. Poor mi gal. Jesus Saviour pilat mi ova life temptestus seas," she said, yawning loudly. "Mi going to mi bed now. Charmaine is aright, is my grip mi using, mi nat using her clean new t'ings pan dat ole dirty bus."

CHAPTER Ten

"I am going to pack now," Timothy said.

"Listen, a quata to four we haffi reach out de cross road. Every mawning de May Flower bus blow roun' a Ben Tree corna 4 o' clock. So right afta Busha leave an' you hear de dog dem bark, dat is when yuh haffi get up," Grandma Hazel instructed Timothy.

"Don't worry Grandma, I will set the clock to alarm 3 o' clock," Timothy replied.

"An' if de clock nuh alarm wah happen?" Grandma asked. "Maas Busha crosses truck mus' mek noise, 'im maingy dog dem always bark, but de dead clock nuh always alarm."

"What if Maas Busha and his dogs dead?" Timothy asked.

"Except you an' yuh pa plan fi kill dem," Grandma Hazel answered, walking away to her room.

Grandma Hazel kept packing and repacking until the cock started crowing. "Firs' cock crow an' mi nuh gone a mi bed yet... mi nat gwine sit here til secon' cock crow an' de bus lef' mi." She finally knelt to pray and was soon fast asleep.

Grandma Hazel was awakened by the loud noise from the alarm clock. Timothy was still fast asleep. "De dead clock alarm, an' I nuh hear neida Mass Busha noisy truck, nor 'im dog dem bark, ah wonda if 'im not going out today," Grandma Hazel said. Just then the dogs started barking loudly, and the noise from Busha's truck engine could be heard. The rooster was crowing again.

"Timoty! Timoty! Bwoy wake up! What a bwoy fi sleep dead," she said. She shook him by the shoulder. "Secon' cock crow, de dead clock alarm, Busha dog an' 'im truck mek one hell of a noise an' yuh still cah wake up."

Timothy jumped out of bed. "I'm awake Grandma," he said, his red eyes bulging.

As soon as they got close to the cross road a bus sped by blowing its horn loudly. "Jesus hab mercy, nuh de confounded bus dat fly pass," said Grandma Hazel. "All because a dis dead bwoy. Any bady si mi trial ya." Her voice touched with heart break. She stood looking at Timothy tragically. Timothy was fearful. "My God, what mi gwine do now?" she asked.

Timothy took a few steps back ward from her. "We could take one of the mini buses Grandma," he suggested.

"Yu hab money fi pay mini bus?" she asked, her words frozen. "What a dissappintment."

Grandma Hazel picked up her grip and taking very slow steps, she said, "Ebry disappointment a fi good. Yuh haffi go an' sen' anada telegram to Lorna as de pos' office open."

"E-mail Grandma, remember," Timothy bravely reminded her.

Grandma Hazel became furious. She was walking faster than she had ever walked. "Is de devil in de confounded net put crosses..." she paused, and her mouth and eyes popped open. "Nuh de bus dat blowin' roun' de corna," she said, as she quickened her pace.

The bus stopped. "Tek yuh time Granny," the bus conductor said, as he helped Grandma Hazel into the bus. "Move it driva!" he shouted, hitting the bus door while hanging on to the door with one hand and dangling one leg out of the bus and puffing on a cigarette. "Town mi a go! Bag Walk! Spanish Town! Saint Cathrine!" he shouted most of the way.

He fussed with the passengers, throwing a few fists on a passenger who refused to pay and used foul language to passengers who would not get into the bus quickly enough for him, even when there was no space. Ten or more passengers had to get out of the bus in order to let one passenger in, then get back into the bus. He even had to flash his 'rachit knife' at a pick pocket who attempted to pick a lady's purse and he called to the driver for a few stops for passengers who needed to use the bush as a latrine.

Passengers were shouting and screaming, as the overcrowded bus leaned to one side while going around the deep bend of the narrow road overlooking the deep valleys and rivers.

When the bus was about to enter Spanish Town, some of the passengers were hiding away marijuana, in preparation for the police raid. The conductor from another bus going in the opposite direction had shouted, "Beas'! Beas'! All who ha ganja oonuh betta hide eh good. De beas' dem swarm Spanish Town." Grandma Hazel had no idea what was going on.

The bus came to a stop in Spanish Town to let off and take on passengers. Four police officers came on board the bus. They made a thorough search for marijuana. A middle-aged lady with an oversized bosom was sitting in the back corner seat. A police officer walked up to her. "Lady, empty yuh bosom," he commanded. "Yuh look overloaded."

"Mi sah?" the lady asked.

"Yes, you," the officer answered.

"But any bady si mi trial ya Pupa Jesus?" the lady said in a pitiable voice while emptying her bosom of keys, thread bags of money secured to her brassiere strap with huge safety pins, a pack of cigarettes and a lighter, a paper bag of mint and a small bundle of freshly cut rosemary.

The officer examined the rosemary thoroughly.

"A rosemary sah," the lady quickly informed the officer.

"What yuh doing with rosemary in yuh bosom lady?" he asked.

"A fi put wid mi money sah so dat de ada higgla dem nuh kip dung mi sale sah. Any time mi figet fi carry some, mi nuh sell a t'ing sah," replied the lady. She was unbelievably serious. She created a scene. All the other passengers were looking at her as if watching a movie.

Grandma Hazel whispered to Timothy, "Wah happen?"

"De police dem searching fi marijuana, Grandma," he answered.

"De ole woman?" Grandma Hazel asked. "What a disgrace, an' mek every bady looking in de woman bussom so, what a outa ordaness fi hab dis young man a look all bout ena de ole woman private part so."

"Nothing is private anymore Grandma, most of the women are wearing low front blouse now, even the older women dem. That is the latest style now, Grandma."

Grandma Hazel looked at her blouse neck, making sure it was buttoned up to the top. The officer glanced at Grandma Hazel but continued his search. She muttered, "'Im nuh badda look pan mi for mi nuh hab a God t'ing deh a hide."

There was loud laughter and arguments from some of the passengers. The officers took three passengers with them, and four crocus bags of marijuana that were not claimed by anyone.

"I am just doing my job," the young officer said as he came off the bus and signaled the driver to go. Every one felt free to voice their opinion now that the police were off the bus. The bus drove off.

"Ole streggae bwoy, a somet'ing ima look fi t'ief. A hungry de maga bwoy hungry," one passenger remarked.

"'Im face fava when dog ha mumps," the lady said, as she repacked her bosom. "'Im nah search de yung gal dem a me ole woman ima come search."

"No, ima look de young gal dem. 'Im outa adah fi ask yuh what yuh doing wid rosemerry, afta ano ganja," another passenger said.

"'Im pass outa ada, look at de ole woman 'im search," Grandma Hazel said.

"Some of them sell it too Grandma," Timothy said.

Grandma Hazel held on to her assumption that Timothy was under the influence of marijuana whenever he spoke of modern technology or behaviours that were rather unbelievable to her. "Is dem you buy it fram when yuh use it?" she asked.

Timothy replied, "I don't use it Grandma. You just don't know what is going on in the world around you and you think I am crazy, Grandma."

"Kingston we reach! Kingston! All who nuh kno' town, dis a Kingston! Every bady get off de bus right ya!" the conductor shouted.

Grandma Hazel looked around at the big, congested city that was so different from the country. Timothy saw Emo's car and ran over to where he was. They drove over to where Grandma was standing.

"Emo, this is Grandma. Grandma, this is Emo, mama's fiancé," Timothy said.

"Yuh mada fi what?" Grandma Hazel asked. She scrutinized the young man from head to toe, looking astonished.

Grandma Hazel thought for a while. Oh, Lorna send a taxi, she assumed inwardly.

Emo hugged Grandma Hazel tight. "I heard so much about you Grandma," he said. She was still thinking, who was this white man?

When they reached the house, Lorna came out to greet her. She hugged Grandma Hazel.

"My God! What a big belly, mi hope is a girl," Grandma Hazel said.

"No Grandma, it's a boy," Lorna informed her.

"Yuh not sure, yuh belly have a roun' shape, it should be a girl," Grandma said.

"Yes Grandma, I am sure, the doctor said so," Lorna replied.

"Only God can be sure," Grandma Hazel said.

"There are tests that can tell what gender it is Grandma."

"Nuh believe dem. In my days, yuh only kno' when is boy or girl when de baby baan."

"Not anymore Grandma, modern technology has vastly improved. Every day they discover something new. Grandma, did you know that women can get pregnant now without having sexual contact with a man?" Timothy asked.

Grandma Hazel looked at Timothy distressingly. Pointing her finger at Lorna, she said, "Listen Lorna, mek mi warn yuh fram now, mek sure seh, if a bwoy yuh really going to ha, as soon as 'im mek de firs' cry yuh open yuh eye dem wide on 'im, so dat 'im nuh come up come run 'im self mad like dis one yuh hab. How in de name of God, woman fi get pregnant widout man touch dem?" Grandma Hazel asked.

"It's true Grandma. The doctors are able to do that," Lorna replied.

"Dem kno' how yes. Look how much a dem mi hear seh rape off dem patient," she said.

"Not like that Grandma. They take the sperm from the man and put it in the woman. This is called artificial insemination," Lorna explained.

"All dat madness," Grandma Hazel replied. "Ah only hope is nat dat yuh do. By de way, where is de fada fi de baby?"

"Timothy, why you did not introduce Emo to Grandma?" Lorna asked.

"Yes Mama, I did, he drove us home."

"Wait, wait, wait, de man who drive us here is a white man," Grandma Hazel said.

"That's him," Lorna replied. "He is a very nice man. Wait until you get to know him, he is from Germany."

"Germany or nuh Germany, mi nuh know wha wrong wid yuh, if yuh neva hear seh black an' white mus' nat hab baby togeda dat baby will have one weak side, an' one strong side an' dem eye brow uneven besides dat, if 'im was nice 'im would married you before 'im impregnate yuh," Gandma Hazel said.

"Grandma, do not listen to people, they do not know better, that's why they say these things. Blacks and whites have been marrying long ago and they have healthy children together, also Emo asked me to marry him, but I am not ready yet."

"Ehe, den how yuh ready fi de baby?" Grandma Hazel asked.

"It was not planned Grandma," Lorna replied.

"Timoty neva plan, an' dis one nuh plan, den a when yuh gwine plan, afta yuh done hab children?"

Lorna tried to nip the conversation in the bud. She got up from her seat and walked over to where the bags were. "Grandma, what do you have in all these boxes and basket? And you still carry the old grip?"

"Well, we olda head keep t'ings, you young people trow way every t'ing, an' spend money like when wata run outa tap."

"But Grandma, things change every day, we have to go with the flow of modern technology."

"Yes, an' go wit' de flow a hard work an' sickness, laziness, crime an' pauperization, dat is all I see flowing, look pan dat t'ing Timoty carry 'im clothes in, it look pretty, but it nuh half strong like mi grip dat all a oonuh hab running belly ova. Yuh right here, mek mi show yuh." She took out several bundles of bushes then instructed Lorna how to use them. "Dis to boil your bath, nine day afta de baby born; dis fi drink fi nine day fi clean yuh out; dis fi de baby drink, one teaspoon fi tree day dat if it swallow any of de head wata, it clean it out. Dis one mek yuh womb go back up quick, quick an' dis one, when yuh feel de firs' pain, yuh drink it. It name 'marratan bush'. Weda de baby come out head or foot firs', or even if de head big like de world atlas, dat baby will run out fass like when yuh pap w'ip bahine jackass. Last but nat leas', dis one name 'cow breas' bush', it mek milk run out a yuh breas' like when dam burse. Oh, dis plastic bag hab piece a string, I boil it, is to tie de baby navel string quick before air get inna it, mi nuh want de navel big."

"Umbilical cord is the right name Grandma," Timothy said.

"'Be like us' or 'nuh be like us', a navel string me know it name. Dem change de name a every God t'ing."

Timothy picked up a plastic bag. "Why you bring sheet Gandma?"

"Sheet?" she asked, snatching the bag from Timothy. "Dese a some nappy from yuh mada was a baby. I bleach dem out on zinc, dem clean, only look a little discolored because dem lock up in de trunk fi t'irty two years." Timothy and Lorna looked at each other in amazement.

Lorna hugged Grandma Hazel. "Grandma, I am so sorry you gave yourself all this trouble."

"Trouble!" she exclaimed, "dat wasn't any trouble, mi glad mi still able to help out."

Lorna sighed, then kissed her. "You are the best."

"Yes mi dalin," said Grandma Hazel, hugging Lorna tighter.

"Just want to tell you something. I really appreciate all that you have done, but I will not be able to use everything. We do not use cloth diapers anymore."

"Den wait a minute, what oonuh use?" she asked.

"We use disposables," Lorna answered.

Grandma Hazel's eyes and mouth popped open. "Dis what?" she asked.

"We use the diapers that we throw away."

"Oonuh betta dan mi, oonuh mussi ha money tree. Mi still si people a country clothes line full a diapa ebry day," Grandma Hazel told her.

"They have time to wash them," Lorna replied.

"Plain lazy, plain lazy," Grandma Hazel remarked. "Well, I will keep dem jus' in case. If de store dem run short mek mi si if yuh would wrap up 'im battam inna bread bag." Grandma Hazel laced the diapers back inside the grip.

"You are right, I better keep them just in case."

"Oonuh caa even t'ink fi oonuh self," Grandma Hazel said. "How yuh going to keep all dis food? I dry de cow tripe over smoke, dem mussi touch by now."

"Mama not going to eat dem if dem touch, Grandma. If not, she will keep them fresh in the refrigerator," Timothy replied.

"You mean keep dem wet... my God oonuh an' oonuh civilization an' modern foolishness. De fridge tek away de good flavor, dats why when mi cook, yuh can stay all de way a town smell it. Yuh seh yuh cooking curry chicken fi dinna an' as near as I am to de kitchen I don't smell a t'ing," she said.

"Grandma, when people get older their sense of smell does not function as it would when they young or middle aged," Lorna said.

"Oh, me ole now so mi caa smell?" Grandma Hazel asked. "De only t'ing I caa smell is oonuh cooking."

"Grandma, we have to get ready to go shopping, today is Saturday," Lorna said.

"Is de gentleman driving?" Grandma Hazel asked.

"No Grandma, I am," replied Lorna.

"You caa drive a God tall, yuh wi ha miscarriage."

"Relax Grandma, I will be ok," Lorna reassured her.

Grandma Hazel's attention was drawn to Timothy's shirt. She gazed for a while, then she asked, "Why yuh change Timoty las' name? I neva know de gentleman adopt him?"

Lorna and Timothy seemed lost since they could not figure out why Grandma Hazel asked such a question.

Grandma Hazel continued, "So a Hell Fighter 'im name? Whata way white people name funny, 'im musbe related to Busha for a de same name mi si Busha shaggy head son hab on 'im shirt, 'im trousers, 'im cap an' even' 'im shoes. Me neva know people start print dem name on dem clothes now, musbe because people get so t'ief nowa days. If yuh no mine sharp dem t'ief yuh eye out yuh head, dem betta start write dem name on dem eye."

Timothy explained. "Grandma, I am wearing a name brand shirt, this is not my name."

"Mi nuh know a God word what yuh talking about," she said.

Lorna explained. "Ok Grandma, some merchandise carry the name of the person who design it, or a given name. The name on Timothy's shirt is Tommy Hilfiger."

Grandma Hazel pointed her finger at Lorna, displaying a serious countenance. She warned Lorna, "Yuh betta leave dat white man alone, because any bady wid dat name caa good, an' mi know Busha ha some good ways, but 'im shoot de chicken outa de egg if it roll pass 'im plantation."

"Things with certain name brands are more costly than others," Lorna eplained.

"Poor mi gal," Grandma Hazel relaxed in her seat. "Lawd Jesus, poor mi gal," she repeated.

Lorna fastened Grandma Hazel's seat belt. "Den why yuh strap mi down? Yuh t'ink mi a mad woman now?"

"No Grandma, if I have to stop suddenly, it prevents us from going through the windshield," Lorna replied.

"Seat belts save many lives," Timothy added. They reached the supermarket and went inside. Timothy pushed the wheel chair with Grandma Hazel while picking up the items that she wanted. She had fun observing other shoppers and she enjoyed the new environment.

Lorna drove up her driveway. The garage door opened automatically. Grandma Hazel bent forward, her mouth open. "De young man was looking out fi yuh," she said.

"Where is he Grandma?" Lorna asked. "He should be at work."

"Nuh 'im open de garage door, but I don't see 'im," said Grandma Hazel, still looking around.

"Oh no, Grandma, it opens automatically. I pressed this button," she said. Lorna and Timothy then took the groceries inside.

Grandma Hazel suddenly shrieked, her eyes wide, She was looking around when she heard a voice say "door ajar". She hobbled indoors as fast as she could. "Lorna! Lorna!" she shouted. "Although me hard a hearing, I could swear I hear a man voice seh 'poor some tar'. It look like somebody lock up inna de car trunk, musbe t'ief. De retch mussi plan fi t'row tar on wi an' rob wi."

"Grandma, calm down honey. The car has an automatic device that tells us when the car door is open," Lorna informed her.

Grandma looked up at the skies. "Jesus, yuh coming soon. Yuh seh at de end of time we will see signs an' wonders. Mi live fi hear car talk an' some human being caa even talk, but I forget seh in Jesus time, de donkey did talk to a man. So in de beginning, so in de end."

"Ok Grandma," Timothy said, "you have not seen signs and wonders yet. Come and sit here let me show you something. It is really not signs and wonders to me Grandma, it is modern technology. It's nothing to hurt you Grandma," Timothy reassured her. "This is the computer I was telling you about that—"

Grandma Hazel became angry and walked away, pointing her finger at Timothy as she said, "Listen bwoy, I tell yuh I ha nat one blessed t'ing to do wid oonuh confounded crosses net. Nuh mek me an' you hab any t'ing, yuh hear mi bwoy!"

Lorna asked, "What is going on?"

Grandma Hazel replied, "If mi did know seh yuh ha dis devil business here, I would neva come."

"What is Grandma talking about Timothy?" Lorna asked.

"Grandma thinks the computer is a devil thing," Timothy replied.

Lorna hugged her. "Come Grandma, I thought you had gotten over this. Would you like to see Charmaine and talk to her?"

"Dat would be a joy, but I don't t'ink Charmaine coming out here for now, maybe not till Christmas," she replied.

"Grandma, you can talk to her on the Internet while you are here and guess what? You can see her too."

Curiosity permeated Grandma Hazel's face. She said, "Oh, it seem like yuh hiding something fram me."

Timothy was bursting with anxiety.

"Wait a minute, yuh ha Charmaine hiding here fi surprise me?" she asked. She had an unforgettable smile on her face, her eyes searching all over.

"Let me explain this to you Grandma." Lorna sat closer to Grandma Hazel, hugging her while trying to reassure her.

Grandma Hazel was still apprehensive. When she saw Charmaine appear on the screen and heard "Hello mother," she gave a look of terrified inquiry. Charmaine said, "Yes mother, I can see you, just the same way you are seeing me. Talk to me, Mom."

"Mercy! Hello dalin," Grandma Hazel replied. She was smiling and waving her hand. Words froze in her mouth for a while before she managed to hold a good conversation with her daughter.

"Now Grandma, while you are here, I would like us to watch TV together. I also planned to send a TV home with you so that you can have some fun and know what is going on in the world around you. I would have to get electricity for you, and Timothy could have a computer to do his school work while he is there with you for the holidays. You could see me and Charmaine and the baby and chat to us whenever you want," said Lorna, trying to convince her.

Grandma Hazel was silent. Glancing at Lorna, she said, "I dont like de electric business at all, next t'ing ebry where burn down. De TV not too bad, but when it come to dat in- de- net business, bwoy, ehe! Anancy seh him nuh trus' no shadow afta dark. Well, me nuh trus' notin in de daylight, afta dark, before dark, nor notin electric."

"Ok Grandma, you think about it, I am going to bed."

The door opened. It was Emo. "Hello! Hello! Hello Grandma," he said, hugging and kissing her. "Are you having a good time honey?" he asked. Grandma Hazel smiled pleasingly, then gave a shy glance. She did not understand his deep German accent. "I will be back to talk to you Grandma," he said. He hacked some phlegm from his throat, shooting it through the window. He walked fast down the hallway.

"Good God," Grandma Hazel said as she made a scornful face. "'Im sick mi stomach, spit right trough de window in front a mi face. Dat white bahine bwoy nuh ha no mannas."

Emo came back with a glass of milk and cookies on a tray. "Here Grandma," he said, after tasting the milk. "Yummy, yummy." He smacked his lips.

"Oh, my belly full sah, but t'ank you, I will have it later," she said.

"No problem Grandma," Emo replied.

"Nasty. 'Im nuh even wash 'im han', den 'im jus' spit an' dip 'im dirty mouth inna de glass. 'Im seem to be a nice fella, but mi caa stan de nastiness," Grandma Hazel muttered.

CHAPTER
Eleven

Grandma Hazel was tired of sitting on the front verandah. She decided to sit in the backyard where the air was fresh and cool. She was on the deck overlooking the swimming pool, surrounded by beautiful flowering trees and plants. She looked at the swimming pool. Wait a minute, she thought, how dis tank wata so blue? Her attention was drawn by a loud splash.

"Jesus Saviour!" she shouted. She walked back indoors as fast as she could. "Mista Emo! Mista Emo! Oh God! Help!" She tried to speak loudly, but her tremulous voice faded. She hit the door with her walking stick. Emo came running from the front verandah. "Somebody flattering in de tank," she said.

Emo held Grandma's hand. "The what?" he asked.

"De tank," she answered. Emo did not understand.

"Oh God," Grandma Hazel said, pointing her stick towards the back door. "Come, run."

Emo came through the door. Timothy was walking around the deck. "What happen Tim?" Emo asked.

"You fall down inna de tank a while ago Timoty?" Grandma Hazel asked.

"No Grandma, this is a swimming pool, I was swimming."

Emo threw himself in a chair and rubbed his head. "Grandma, would you like to go in the pool?" he asked.

"Mi, mi fi go inna swimming school in fi mi ole age yah? No sah!" Grandma Hazel answered.

Timothy clarified, "Not school Grandma, pool."

"What yuh seh bwoy?" She raised her stick at Timothy. "Yuh call mi a fool?" Timothy jumped into the pool, making a big splash. Grandma Hazel held her chest.

"Are you hurting, Grandma?" Emo asked.

"No Maas Emo, she is afraid," Timothy replied.

"Well, maybe we could get her to overcome her fear by helping her to get used to the pool," Emo said.

"No Maas Emo, it would be easier to get the light post to walk into the pool, than to get Grandma to go in there," Timothy replied.

"I will take you on my back Grandma," Emo said.

Grandma Hazel became serious. "Listen, when I bade, I full up mi bath pan wit' warm wata, not even riva mi neva bade. Nex' t'ing mi ketch up cole an' ketch consumption. A kill oonuh wa kill mi?" she asked.

"Grandma, remember Busha has a big swimming pool in his back yard," Timothy said.

"Afta mi nat going inna Busha back yawd," she replied.

Emo was communicating with his eyes most of the time, as he did not understand most of what was being said. Grandma Hazel was accustomed to reading her bible and praying at special times of the day, and even though she was away from home she would not dare to disregard her fellowship with God. She remembered and right away gave Timothy instructions.

"Timoty, please go inside an' bring mi bible an' spectacle."

Timothy was on his way, when suddenly he shouted, "Grandma! Grandma! Mama is going to have the baby!"

"Have mercy my God!" Grandma Hazel said. She tried to get up quickly, but staggered back onto the bench. She grabbed her stick and headed indoors. Lorna was holding her stomach. Her face was contorted. "Lawd Jesus, poor t'ing, lay down let mi si if de baby head showing," Grandma Hazel said.

"Crowning, Grandma, crowning," Timothy corrected her, as he usually did.

"Bwoy go bout yuh business, in a serious time like now, yuh choose fi talk foolishness. Where yuh eva si baby born wit' crown on dem head?" Grandma Hazel asked.

Emo came running; he was jumping around in a circle, shouting, "My baby! My baby is coming!"

Grandma looked at him and thought: "My God, a life an' death situation right now, an' 'im hab time fi jump roun' inna circle like John Crow picking dead meat."

She then shouted, "Timoty! Bring de grip wid de things an' run go call de midwife." Grandma Hazel quickly put on her white linen apron. Lorna shook her head in pity though she appreciated her care and concern. It was hard to disappoint her. She gave Grandma Hazel a hug and asked her kindly to sit with her until Emo came back.

"Grandma, Emo will drive me to the hospital, I am ok."

"Hospital!" Grandma Hazel shouted. "Yuh mean in a big city like dis dem don't hab midwife?"

"It's ok Grandma, I prefer to go to the hospital."

Grandma Hazel was not listening to a word of what Lorna was saying. "Timoty, put some wata on de fiah, an' tek out de plastic bag wid de string an' tek out de bush mark 'marratan' an' put it inna de pot," she ordered. She was ready to be the midwife.

"Grandma, nobody use those things any more, and the bush may be contraindicated with the medicines," Timothy said.

Grandma Hazel did not understand what Timothy meant. "Seh wah? De bush will mek she contract in de gate? Den nuh all de betta, de baby would come quick den maybe she could avoid going in de hospital."

"Never mind Grandma," Timothy said.

Emo lifted Lorna into the car.

Grandma Hazel gave a sigh of relief, though she did not like to hear about the hospital. She looked at Emo pleasingly. "How dem seh white people weak? Dem strong," she said. She picked up her grip when no one was looking.

Every groan Lorna made, Grandma Hazel returned an unconscious groan. "Hurry masa, but please be careful," Grandma Hazel said.

"We are almost there honey, everything is going to be alright," Emo reassured her.

Grandma Hazel began to pray as tears trickled down her cheeks. Lorna was escorted to the labour unit by a tall porter. He pushed his way through the crowd of people, who were anxiously waiting to get through the iron gates that were controlled by security guards. The porter shouted, "Coming through! Coming through! Clear the way!"

"Why do you look so sad?" the porter asked. "Don't worry man, everything will be alright." Everyone seemed surprised as his approach superceeded his countenance. Grandma Hazel's face relaxed. "You sweet little lady, don't be so sad, we will take good care of her," said the porter as he continued to push his way through the crowd.

"Coming through! Coming through!" he shouted. Some people didn't move, they were standing and looking bewildered like goats, while others cleared the entrance.

"Who is the next of kin?" the porter asked.

Timothy, Grandma Hazel, and Emo were following him. "Cuyah God, what 'im seh, who fah neck hab skin?" Grandma Hazel asked. "Ebry body neck hab skin."

"Shhh," Timothy said. Emo stepped forward.

The porter said, "Grandma, youth, you can't come in. What is in this grip?"

Grandma Hazel answered, "De string to tie de baby navel string, nappy an' belly ban' fi de baby an' my grand daughter sah." The porter shook his head and went to get the nurse.

A middle-aged nurse walked briskly to the door. Sweat was running down her face and neck. "You cannot come in yet honey, and we do not use these things any more."

There was a loud "Ooooooo! Nurse, nurse! Ooooo, mi belly!" coming from the labour ward. The nurse spun back to the ward.

Grandma Hazel walked away feeling disappointed. "Poor mi gal," she said, giving a distressful sigh.

There was a lady standing in the corner observing all that was going on and interfering in every one's business. She said, "Lawd ha mercy, sweat a run offa de nurse like she a go trough menopause."

Grandma Hazel asked, "Parden mi darling, men do wah?"

"Ah seh de nurse look like she a go trough change a life," the lady rephrased.

"Oh," Grandma Hazel replied, smiling. "Where she come fram nuh know fi eat yam, mi eat so much yam. Mi neva know when change a life go trough nor come trough."

"Now a days dem hab so many different pills fi help menapause, Grandma," the lady replied.

"An' ask if de pill dem nuh mek dem pass," Grandma Hazel said.

"A true ma," she replied.

A tall, thinly built young woman was walking past Grandma Hazel. She looked at Grandma Hazel's grip and laughed mockingly. "Kiss mi neck, mi neva know seh Dulsimena grip still inna fashion."

A bystander intervened. "Lef' de little ole lady, and go bout yuh business," he said.

Timothy stepped up to her, pointing in her face. "Watch it streggae! This is my great grandmother."

The woman asked, "A who yuh a call streggae?" Though it was hot, she was wearing a thick, long sleeved, wollen sweater. She started to roll her sleeves up, freeing her arms to fight.

The security guard stood between them to separate them. Grandma Hazel called Timothy away so as to avoid the fight.

Timothy said, "Grandma, I told you not to carry that old grip, I thought you left it at home."

"A bright de confounded gal bright," she replied. "A fi mi grip."

"Don't worry Grandma, we have Mama to worry about."

"Daniel God will deliver her, we should not worry when we pray," she replied.

Emo walked back aimlessly. His eyes watery, he started to sob.

"Lawd Jesus, what happen?" Grandma Hazel asked.

Emo was speechless.

"Oh God, nuh tell mi seh dem mek she dead in child birth. Lawd Jesus!" Grandma Hazel shouted, taking a seat on a fire hydrant. She dropped her stick, putting her hands on her head. Timothy's eyes moistened with tears.

"What happen man?" he asked sternly.

"Lorna is, oh God Lorna is..." stuttered Emo.

"Is what?" Timothy asked.

"She is having twins and has to have surgery," Emo replied.

"Man, so what!" shouted Timothy, then he explained to Grandma Hazel.

"Well, my God, 'im almose kill mi. 'Im nuh look like 'im righted," she said. "Mi don't like de operation business at all. But mi glad is nat dead she dead. Is mi she tek de twin genes from. I had twin boys."

"What happen to them Grandma?" Timothy asked.

"Dem died sudden when dem was only two week old. Both a dem foam an' jus' stiff dead," replied Grandma Hazel.

"That's called S.I.D.S., Grandma," said Timothy.

"Seed, what kina seed? Afta dem couldn't eat yet," she said.

"I said S.I.D.S. Grandma, not seeds. S.I.D.S. means Sudden Infant Death Syndrome. That's when an infant dies suddenly of an unknown cause."

"Maasa shut yuh mout', yuh a yung bud. A spirit play wid dem. My gran fada dead two weeks before dem born. Eida 'im feed dem or play wid dem," she said.

"Spirits have no power, Grandma," Timothy replied. "It was S.I.D.S. or they aspirated."

"Me nuh know what yuh talking bout sudden infant deh drown, or dem expirate, I neva even put dem in basin when I bade dem. I spread plastic an' towel on de bed an' bade dem on it. How dem fi drown on plastic or towel?" she asked. "It seem like even when yuh nuh get fi smoke dat bush, yuh head still tek yuh."

There was a sudden downpour of rain that forced every one to seek shelter. Some were opening umbrellas and newspapers over their heads. Grandma Hazel, Timothy and Emo sat on a bench close to the surgical area. Grandma Hazel was praying. Emo looked as if he was beaten by the wind, his hair stood straight up like thorns. Timothy was listening to his music. The porter who had wheeled Lorna in, was passing by and stopped. "Is everything ok?" he asked.

"She has to have surgery, she is having twins," replied Timothy.

He looked surprised. "Surgery!"

"I don't like de operation at all," said Grandma Hazel, her voice dampened with tears.

"We have some good surgeons here, I will check to see which one is on duty, I think is Surgeon Death," he said. Everyone's attention was drawn to the porter.

"Surgeon Death!" Timothy exclaimed. "You are joking, right?"

A student nurse was passing by. "Why is everyone so sad? Did someone die?" she asked.

"No, no. Her granddaughter is having surgery," the porter answered. "Tell me something, which of de surgeons on duty today?"

"Surgeon De Wayne and Surgeon Deptasengali. They are both very good, don't worry, she will be fine," she reassured them.

"I seem to pronounce the name wrong," said the porter.

There was a loud whistling from the bend of the corridor. A young porter was walking towards the building. He suddenly stopped. His eyes fixed on his colleague. He said, "But you nuh easy to blouse an' skirt, look how much people out deh inna wheel chair a wait, an' you stan' up out ya a tell anancy story. What, you t'ink de white bwoy have money fi give you? You nuh si seh a dulsimena grip ima carry? 'Im caa even afford to buy a good suitcase. A musa boat dem trow 'im outa an' 'im swim ashore."

"Gwaan man, yuh love fass wid people. Dats why yuh a walk like tree foot goat," said the middle-aged porter. He hissed his teeth as he walked away.

Emo asked, "Timothy, will you take this grip and put it in the trunk of the car?"

"No way," Timothy replied, walking away.

"Put it here beside mi," said Grandma Hazel, "mi nuh shame a mi grip."

Emo placed the grip beside Grandma Hazel. "I am going to check on Lorna," he said.

Along came an emaciated looking, middle-aged woman. She had a face no one would envy. She looked at the grip, then looked at Grandma Hazel. She opened a container filled with rice and peas and chicken and cabbage that was enough to feed a family of four. The stale aroma filled the air. She hurriedly ate as though someone was coming to take the food from her. She belched loudly, causing Grandma Hazel to shake from fear. The woman laughed.

"Heh, hehe, heh, aaa, yuh easy fi frighen eh? Mannas," she said, then looked at the grip again, looked at Grandma Hazel and walked away shaking her head.

CHAPTER Twelve

Emo came back looking pleased. "Good news?" Grandma Hazel asked.

"Neither good nor bad," he answered. The sun was shining brightly and Grandma Hazel was sweating profusely.

"Kingston hotta dan de country," she said.

"Because there are more trees in the country," Emo replied.

"Maas Emo, please if yuh could go an' buy a erated wata fi mi. Buy ginga ale," she said, reaching in her bossom to take money from her thread bag.

"It's ok Grandma, I will pay for it," said Emo. He stopped at the little booth that was operated by two rasta men. "Please, may I have a bottle of era, era, erated water, ginger ale?" he asked.

"Erated wata! You mean soda, iah?" the rasta man asked. His eyes met with his partner who was chipping ice.

"I guess so," Emo replied.

As Emo walked away, the rasta man said, "A whea de blouse an' skirt dis ya white bredda come fram? 'Im mussi escape outa fada Noah ark. Jah help 'im fi escape cross de rivas of Babylan an' 'im lan' pon I an' I fada creation, Jah!" he shouted, kicking his legs in the air like a ram goat frightened by thunder.

The nurse came out smiling. "You have a beautiful package," she said. Neither Grandma Hazel nor Emo realized what the nurse meant when she mentioned 'package'.

Lorna had twin boys and was in the recovery room. Everyone was happy, especially Grandma Hazel who had been so worried about losing her granddaughter in childbirth.

When they got home, they were all excited.

"You name de baby dem yet?" Grandma Hazel asked.

"Tamar and Trevor," said Timothy.

"Call dem James and John," said Grandma Hazel.

Emo thought for a while. "Their names will be Liem Tamar James Zimmerman and Kiefer Trevor John Zimmerman, so we all get to name them." Emo was well known to be a compassionate young man who tried to please everyone. "Your last name is Zimmerman?" Timothy asked. "What a long name."

"Yes it's German, meaning carpenter," he replied.

"I see, so yuh is a carpenta?" Grandma Hazel asked.

"No Grandma, I am an electrical engineer, a tailor and also a photographer," he replied.

"Jack of all trade," said Grandma Hazel.

"Which is your main job?" Timothy asked.

"Whatever is available at any given time," replied Emo. "That way, I will always be working."

"Well, mama should be home in a few days," said Timothy.

"You mean weeks," said Grandma Hazel, who was not thinking that things had changed.

"No Grandma, it should be about four days. If she

had normal delivery, it would be only two days," replied Timothy.

"Seh what! In my days we stay in nine days wit' de window an' door dem shut tight. We could only peep trough hole an' when de door open, we shet it back quick before we ketch up cole," said Grandma Hazel.

"Not any more Grandma," said Timothy.

"I am going to e-mail Aunt Charmaine to tell her the good news."

"She is not your aunt, she is your grandmother," said Emo.

"Yes, she is my grandmother but I call her Aunt Charmaine because she is still young," replied Timothy.

"Nuh turn on dat 666 machine in here, de new baby dem coming home," said Grandma Hazel.

"It's ok, Grandma," Emo said, patting her on the shoulder.

Lorna and her babies were home at last. Grandma Hazel was busy with the twins. She insisted that they wore belly bands. Lorna allowed her to put them on to make her happy. Grandma fed the babies. "Come Timoty, wash de bottle an' boil it," she ordered him.

"No Grandma, we throw them in the garbage. We cannot use them twice, they are called disposables," he told her.

Grandma Hazel became angry. "Bwoy, yuh caa come near dese baby, stop chat madness a mi ears bwoy, how yuh mus' trow weh de bottle?"

"Yes Grandma, they should only be used one time, they are disposable," said Lorna.

Grandma Hazel took a deep breath. "My God, inna fi mi time, we could only afford one bottle, dose time was only plastic. Even when de nipple hole wide like Willy penny, we haffi still use it. We boil it till de colour bid goodbye. Some people use to use erated wata bottle an' barely tilt it. De baby suck an' suck till dem jaw tiad, or dem choke because too much go in dem mout' one time. Now oonuh trow weh nappy, bottle an' ebry t'ing. Oonuh soon trow weh de poor baby dem tinking dem disposable too. Wit' oonuh madness," she concluded.

CHAPTER
Thirteen

Time went by and Grandma Hazel had many adventures, even adapting to some modern technology. She became home sick. She missed her animals, friends, her old country church worship, and also the children in the village. Timothy and his great grandmother prepared to travel back home. She made sure she did not leave her grip even though Lorna bought new luggage. "I wish you would stay longer," said Lorna and Emo. "We are glad you came, Grandma." They hugged and kissed goodbye. "Your next trip will be to America," Lorna told her.

Grandma Hazel gave a daring look and then smiled. "Only if bus can carry me dere," she replied.

The conductor signaled the driver to drive by blowing his whistle and hitting on the side of the bus as hard as he could. He was hanging on to the bus with one hand while searching for more passengers though the bus was already overfilled and some passengers were standing on the bus steps. The overcrowded bus gave a puff of smoke and drove off slowly.

"One stop driver!" shouted a passenger, trying to squeeze her way out of the crowded bus.

"Daughta, nex' time walk go weh yuh a go, yuh nuh seet, de bus jus' drive off an' yuh want stop aready," the conductor said angrily. He tried to overcharge the lady, but was not successful so he unleashed a few curse words. Then he signaled the driver to go while he shouted, "St. Cathrine! Spanish Town! Linstead! Browns Town we a go!"

"One stop driva!" he yelled.

"Stop driva! Yuh deaf?" shouted some of the passengers.

"Step pan it driva, 'im musa gwine put dem pan' 'im head fi sidung," uttered a higgler lady. "'Im nuh si seh de half dead bus full."

"Weeeee!" sounded the whistle. A middle-aged woman was running breathlessly. She was held back by the weight of her over-sized chest.

"Run fatty!" said the conductor, stretching out his hand and pulling her into the bus while signaling the driver to go before she even got inside the bus. He grabbed on to her and pushed her in front of him. "Move dung inna de bus!" he shouted, stretching his stringy arms to help keep the woman from falling out of the bus. The unpleasant aroma of his sweaty body blended in with the already combustable air.

"Step dung! Move it!" he shouted, forcing his way through the overcrowded bus, trying to make space for more passengers.

"Ooooo! Oh God!" a woman screamed. "De pig bwoy step pan mi corn toe." She lifted her foot out of her slippers. The young man continued forcing his way through the bus.

"And de bwoy nuh have no mannas. 'Im nat even look back much less fi seh 'im sorry," said a passenger.

"Sorry fi wha? Yuh si man a pass, yuh shudda move outa de way!" shouted the young man from the opposite end of the bus.

"Which part ah yuh a man? Yuh hungry, ill mannad retch, ah hope yuh nuh sidung a de back a de bus an' nyam out de passinga dem food," said the lady.

While Grandma Hazel was busy thinking about her adventures, her attention was drawn by what the lady said about the conductor eating the passengers' food. "Ah only hope to God 'im nuh nyam out de little fry sprat what Lorna give mi," she muttered, displaying a perplexed look on her face.

"Don't worry Grandma. The way I tie the box, he will not bother to open it," Timothy reassured her.

After a long and uncomfortable journey, Grandma Hazel and Timothy finally reached home. She was happy to see her fowls and rabbits. She rewarded Raymet for taking such good care of them. Grandma Hazel said, "Timoty, ah will haffi write Lorna before ah go to bed, an' yuh drop de letter a de post office, as soon as it open."

"You don't have to do that Grandma. I have a cell phone," said Tomothy.

"Who sell phone, where mi mus' get money fi buy phone? Mi neva ask yuh who sell phone," said Grandma Hazel. "Something wrong wid yuh?" she asked as she walked away.

Timothy walked behind her. He insisted on trying to convince her. "Look Grandma, this is a cell phone, I am calling mama now, watch me." Timothy started to dial the number. Grandma Hazel hised her teeth and walked faster.

She turned around, pointing her finger at Timothy. She said, "Ah de same t'ing ah si even de babe on suckling wit' phone at dem ears upa town."

"Down here too Grandma," Timothy added.

"Well, mi nuh want none a dem hell boun' devil tool inna fi mi house, next t'ing de house blow up in flame wid wi. If mi did want fi burn inna fiah, I would'nt live a Christian life all dese years, I would live fi de devil."

There was a strange sound outside as if someone was counting slowly. Timothy looked through the window, it was Miss Dassa and Maas Freddie. Miss Dassa was humming. She shouted, "Hay Hay! Lawd Hay Hay! Yuh come back?"

"Yes mi dear Miss Dassa, mi neva get here till 3 o'clock. De 'May Reach' bus stop stop ebry minute. De bus pack so till it look like de baggage bwoy put some a de people dem on tap a de bus," said Grandma Hazel.

"Lawd Hay Hay, yuh look good, yuh put on some flesh ma. What a way de Kingston breeze gree wid yuh," Maas Freddie said.

"Yes mi dear sah," she replied, "dem tek good care a mi, even de red skin German man."

Miss Dassa and her husband looked surprised. "German man? A German man Lana go put her self wid?"

"He seem to be a nice young man," replied Grandma Hazel.

"Mi hear seh dem rough ma," said Miss Dassa.

"Me to," said Maas Freddie.

"Den, Hay Hay, yuh carry back one young man fi mi?" Miss Dassa asked.

"Mi nuh t'ink yuh want trouble in yuh life ma, dem full a problem," answered Grandma Hazel.

"A wha yuh a talk bout young man? Yuh caa even manage me an' look how me ole," said Maas Freddie.

"Manage yuh, a wha yuh ha fi manage?" Miss Dassa asked, looking at Maas Freddie from the corner of her eyes. "Fi yuh manhood tun babyhood long time."

Timothy asked, "Miss Dassa, what are you talking about?"

"None a yuh business," she answered. "Freddie know what mi talking bout." She glanced at Timothy's cell phone. "Hay Hay, yuh mean seh yuh mek de bwoy carry da hell phone inna yuh house?"

"Yuh neva call anyt'ing by the right name," said Maas Freddie. "De right name is scandal line."

"Dat musbe de nick name people give it because mose people use it fi chat people business," said Miss Dassa.

"Ah tell 'im ah dont want dat t'ing in here fi blow up mi house," said Grandma Hazel.

"Mi nuh t'ink it can blow up de house, but mi t'ink it can blow up people head. Mi hear seh people get bump in dem head; dat something what mek dem head big. Yes, yes dem call it bluma, or, a, oh, tuma, docta haffi cut dem head inna two an' tek it out. Some a dem turn idiot," said Miss Dassa.

"Oh boy," said Timothy, giving Miss Dassa a sarcastic look.

Grandma Hazel said, "Ebry t'ing dat Lorna see she run go buy it give 'im, even de two week ole baby dem mussi ha one."

"Seh wha!" shouted Maas Freddie. "Yuh mean de baby dem wha Lorna jus' hab?" His mouth and eyes popped open wide.

"Lawd Freddie yuh a idiot an' yuh nuh use hell phone. How four week ole baby fi use hell phone?" Miss Dassa asked, looking at her husband incredulously.

"De bible seh, there will be signs an' wandas when 'im near to come for 'im world," said Maas Freddie.

"Double idiot," grumbled Timothy as he walked away.

Grandma Hazel said, "Talking bout phone, yuh will neva believe dis, dem mek mi go in de net."

"Seh wha ma!" shouted Miss Dassa.

Grandma Hazel continued. "Den I stay right in de net in Kingston an' see mi daughta all de way in America an' even talk to her."

Miss Dassa rolled her eyes. "Hay Hay, yuh mean yuh mek dem sweet talk yuh in dat net. Suppose yuh did fine yuh self in

America, because mi hear seh it tek yuh anywhere an' yuh can see anybody anywhere, if yuh hab it set up fi special ways."

"Hay Hay, yuh brave ma. If dem pay mi ten million dalla mi nat going in dat net," said Maas Freddie.

Timothy explained, "It is not a net you go into. You look at a screen like a TV."

"Yes, yes jus' like dat," said Grandma Hazel. "Den Lorna want Timoty to get one. Ah tell her not ova mi dead body. So she go bahine mi back an' give him de phone."

Grandma Hazel told them all about her adventures, the twins and all the changes that she had not been aware of. They sat and ate fried fish and bread and drank hot peppermint tea.

Maas Freddie started to cough. Water ran from his eyes and nostrils. He seemed to have swallowed a scotch bonnet pepper seed. Miss Dassa, not thinking said, "Me neva si a big ole man ack lika pickeny so. Yuh bet a de fish bone turn crossway 'im troat mek 'im a cough lika when dog swalla hot peppa."

Timothy came running with a piece of iron pipe in his hand. "Open your mouth Maas Freddie, I will clear whatever is in your throat." Miss Dassa looked at Timothy then hissed her gum. He left, then came back with a long stalk from a papaya leaf. "Open your mouth Maas Freddie," he said.

"Bwoy, mine yuh damage 'im gall bladda," said Miss Dassa.

"Gall bladder!" said Timothy. "His gall bladder is not in his throat."

"Well a musbe some ada bladda," she said.

"Yuh mean 'im tonsil?" Grandma Hazel asked.

Maas Freddie looked at Grandma Hazel, his eyes protruding in surprise. "Fi mi tonsil gone up inna mi head long time," he said. Timothy fell to the ground laughing. Maas Freddie was serious. "Now tell mi," he asked, "why dat bwoy love laugh afta people so like dem a idiot? Mi kno' dem seh when people get ole dem tonsil migrate in dem head."

"No wanda fi yuh head tek a different shape since yuh get ole. For when mi meet yuh, yuh head neva broad so," Miss Dassa said. Grandma Hazel was dozing off. She was weary, still tired from her trip.

Miss Dassa stood up. "Come Freddie, mek we go home. Hay Hay tiad from her journey, she want to go to her bed." Timothy accompanied them home. Miss Dassa started to close the door then she shouted, "Timoty! Come back here! No carry dat phone inna yuh granma house, yuh hear mi? Put it unda de sella," she warned him, then slammed the heavy wooden door.

Grandma Hazel slept undisturbed all night. She was awakened by the crowing of the rooster and the noise from the woodpecker picking ants from the window sill. She sat on the verandah inhaling the fresh air, and admiring the multicoloured clouds illuminated by the sun that was creeping up behind the hills. The sunflowers opened wider as the butterflies greeted them with a kiss. The fowls gathered around the verandah in a group, milling around. Grandma Hazel got up, clapped her hips and walked off. "A hungry deese miserable retch hungry mek dem swaam de verandah so," she said.

Grandma Hazel fed the fowls and admired her garden. She heard the loud chattering of the children's voices. "Good morning Grandma," they said.

"Hello my little ones," she replied. Her face glowed with a wide smile. The children were suddenly quiet. They were looking around at each other and at Grandma Hazel. Some were digging the ground with the point of their shoe, with their heads held down.

A little girl spoke up loudly. "Grandma Hazel, Angela want neaseberry fi buy ma."

"Mi neva tell yuh so," said Angela, with her head held down.

A little red haired boy ran from behind the house and said, "A sweety we come beg yuh Grandma, for Timoty seh you carry plenty from town."

"Mi hab sweety an' popcorn fi all a yuh but it too early, come back later in de evening," she told them.

"Yeah!" said the boy. They ran through the gate happily.

Timothy was busy talking on his cell phone. Grandma Hazel saw him. "Timoty! All de fun ova now. School soon open an' yuh not even pick up yuh book an' read. When yuh nat in your fren net, yuh sidung wid dat t'ing in yuh han'. All I hear is ping ping, pang pang, zoo zoo. Go look fi yuh school book dem an' get something in yuh tough head!" she shouted.

Timothy replied, "Grandma, all I need to do is go to Donovan's house and practice maths on his computer." Grandma Hazel stood speechless looking at Timothy, her face creased with concern and grief.

"Grandma, you just don't understand," said Timothy.

"Siah bwoy, mi nat going to mek yuh sen' my soul a hell, get up! Go get yuh book! Every t'ing, mi nuh understan', oh, mi tun goat now, get up!" she repeated.

"Grandma you—" Timothy tried to explain. Grandma Hazel grabbed her enamel mug. Timothy fled across the hall faster than a mongoose. "Grandma, I forget to buy my history book," he said.

"Go an' look in de trunk unda de bed yuh will see your mada history book what she use when she was in third grade."

Timothy smiled.

"That is too old Grandma, and that is not the type of history we are studying now, that was years ago," replied Timothy.

"Bwoy, I am nat a fool, history is always ole dat is why dem call it history, but it can neva be too ole."

Timothy explained, "There are different types of history Grandma, and what is in mama book is not what I am studying now."

"It still name history, an' since yuh forget your book, go study it because if your book was important, yuh would neva forget it. If yuh don't want to use your mada history book, go unda de sella, look in de big wooden trunk, yuh see fimi reading book dat I had eighty years ago, read it!" she said. "It says, Dis is Dora, Dora can jump, jump Dora jump, Dis is Ned, Ned has a hat on his head. His head is big, he likes to dig, or, Humpy Dumpy sat on a wall, Humpy Dumpy had a hell of a fall." Timothy laughed loudly.

"That is for babies Grandma, I am a teenager, those were silly books."

Grandma was upset by Timothy's remarks. She stood upright and stared at him.

"Listen bwoy, all when mi a big gal mi still read dem. What is silly, is dem short han' t'ings dem bringing in nowadays what cause oonuh fi caa even spell oonuh name widout using machine. In my days mi haffi repeat page afta page outa my head like when mi gulping dung wata. It was a burden shame, I went to church wit' Lorna an' de whole choir hold dung dem head in de book like dem nuh hab no brain, no wanda gunman breaking in de church dem in de middle day an' rob de whole church offering an' dem not even see dem because dem mostly come in when dem singing all because dem realize dat all of dem hole dung dem head in de book." Grandma continued, "Dere was a little red head bwoy, 'im was as cute as a cat, bout seven year ole, I don't mean seven day old, seven year ole, 'im was taking part in a play, he was to say, my mother Gena. To mi surprise, 'im was reading it off piece of paper, but bigga surprise de bwoy mada real name was Gena. De pickney nuh rememba 'im mada name. 'Im hold up de big sheet a paper fi read only tree wud."

"You don't understand Grandma," Timothy said.

She stood as tall as her aged body allowed her. "What in de name of God mi nuh understan'?" she asked. "Yuh t'ink when people get ole dem grow two more leg, a tail an' two horns sticking outa dem head, dem food change to grass, dem filt look like black pebble, an' dem tie dem unda shady tree an' a bawl baaa, baa?'

"That sounds like goat, Grandma," Timothy replied.

Timothy kept walking around in circles and looking at his watch.

"I have to run to catch the store open Grandma, I need the money that mama is sending," he said. Grandma Hazel opened her mouth and eyes wide.

"Lawd Jesus! Have mercy upan dis mad bwoy!" She raised her arms in the air, requesting help from above. "'Im head gone again. How money fi reach so quick?"

"Mama called five minutes ago and said she send it Grandma."

"How in de name of God! Bwoy mi nah run up mi pressure ova yuh madness for it favor like yuh ha lifetime brain trouble."

"Grandma, the net sends information throughout the world," Timothy informed her.

"So, money walk trough de net from Kingston all de way here, so dat mean people will soon be walking in de net to go anywhere dem want to go," said Grandma Hazel.

"No Grandma, that will never happen," he replied.

"Yuh jus' nuh expose yuh self to dat t'ing too long, jus' tek out de money an' change it fi different money. Store turn in pos' office now?" she asked.

"No Grandma, listen Grandma, there are faster ways to send money now. It only takes a few minutes, any where in the world we have Money Gram, Western Union, and others," he explained.

"Notin but dat net," she concluded. "Yuh jus' hurry an' come back. Mek sure yuh don't carry de same money dat yuh tek out dat net come in here," she warned Timothy.

Timothy came back quickly, sweat was bursting from his pores. "Mama send some extra money. She says we must buy a microwave."

Grandma Hazel looked lost. "Mi caa tek dis crazyness no more, no sah!" she said. "Yuh eva see crow wave? Mek mi smell yuh mouth bwoy."

"Not crow wave Grandma, I said mi-cro-wave," he emphasized. "It is like an oven Grandma."

"Well, why dat name? It soun' like a scavinga oven," she said.

"No Grandma, see like how you love cow foot Grandma, when you are cooking it, instead of taking hours to cook, it will only take minutes."

Grandma Hazel's eyes grew wild with misery. "Mi nuh want notin like dat in here. So, my food mus' cook on de net now?" she asked.

Timothy answered, "It has nothing to do with the Internet Grandma, not again."

"Crow wave or crow net, nuh bring it here!" she shouted. "Mi allow Lorna fi run electricity here, jus' fi satisfy her, but mi nat using it," said Grandma Hazel.

"Not again Grandma," said Timothy, getting annoyed. "Get real Grandma Hazel."

"Bwoy, a yuh an' yuh ma fi get real, what, mi tun duppy before mi dead, mi nuh real?" Grandma Hazel asked furiously. "Mek me go res' mi tiad self." She had ginger tea and crackers, then prepared for a night's rest. She read her bible and prayed, asking God to have mercy on His world that men had changed in so many ways. She dimmed the kerosene lamp, placed her sharp machete close to her bed and was soon asleep.

CHAPTER
Fourteen

The long summer holiday was over. Timothy was back in high school and Grandma Hazel was alone. Timothy visited whenever he got the chance and Lorna and Charmaine also visited as often as they could. Things had changed over the years. The older folks were either moving to live with their relatives or had passed away. Grandma Hazel survived most of her friends. The crime rate was rapidly increasing in the once peaceful island of Jamaica. But even at 95 years old Grandma Hazel was still making sure her machete was sharp and placed close to her bed at nights with the intention of chopping anyone who would try to break into her house.

Lorna went to America for a long vacation. On her return she told Grandma Hazel all about America; how much she enjoyed her stay and would like to visit again. Grandma Hazel realized that people had wrong ideas about life in America. Charmaine kept encouraging her mother to spend time with her, but had no success over the years. Charmaine learned that her mother was becoming lonely and fearful, and soon became anxious to take her chance to visit America. But under one condition, only if Charmaine or Lorna would be willing to travel with her.

Grandma was ready to take on the challenge. Charmaine quickly made arrangements for her to get her passport and visa.

It was a beautiful summer morning when Lorna and Timothy drove home to take Grandma Hazel to the embassy for her visa appointment. Grandma Hazel was experiencing anxiety and fear. "T'ank yuh fadah for protecting us safe," Grandma Hazel whispered under her breath, as soon as Lorna drove up the narrow, graveled driveway which was beautifully decorated on both sides with flowers and white washed rocks.

She had prepared Lorna's favorite dishes, yellow rice, yam, young breadfruit, peppered shrimp, ackee and saltfish, potato pudding and coconut cakes. She still cooked very well, despite her age. Grandma Hazel's face was like a 100 watt bulb as they greeted each other, hugging and kissing. The inquisitive neighbours were peeping out their windows and doors while others made excuses to stop by, trying to find out what was going on. Grandma Hazel took a good look at Lorna from head to toe. "My God, den cloth scarce...yuh caa buy enough? Wat mek your dress so short an' tight or is de style?" Gandma Hazel asked.

"No Grandma, is the style," she replied.

"Good God, do betta dan dat, might as well yuh walk naked. How de gentleman allow yuh to dress like dat?" she asked.

"Oh Grandma, don't worry. He loves when I dress like this."

"Jus' mek sure yuh hab a decent dress to wear when yuh taking me go down at de embassy," said Grandma Hazel. "Poor mi gal, dese new generation come fi tun de world upside down."

"No Grandma, we came to be rulers of tomorrow!" replied Timothy.

"I hope God take me outa dis world before a mad shark like yuh tun ruler," said Grandma Hazel.

Everyone sat on the verandah chatting while enjoying the delicious peppered shrimp. Dogs were barking loudly. The flame of a bright torch could be seen in the distance. Miss Dassa and Maas Freddie came to greet Lorna and to wish them a safe trip. She had some of the peppered shrimp, but Maas Freddie was sorry for his gum so he had a big mug of coffee instead. Miss Dassa smiled at Lorna, and took a long, noisy slurp of coffee. She said, "Lana, ah hope yuh know yuh haffi leave as de day start peep."

"Why? We are driving," replied Timothy.

"Well, mi hear seh de amount a people what go a town fi travel paper, de line lang fram Kingston to Spanish Town. Dem even bill up roadway up to de sky a St. Catherine, dat some of de people dem can stanup, an' yuh dare not come out a de line weada sun ar rain, even if bush call yuh," said Miss Dassa. "What dem call de road what dem build in de sky Freddie?" she asked.

"Aam, aam tru, oh, oh, it name tall road," replied Maas Freddie.

"My God," said Grandma Hazel, cupping her hand over her cheek.

Timothy meaning to be sarcastic, asked, "So, is President Bush call the people? President Bush don't call anyone."

"Bwoy yuh fool fool like goat, mi mean even if yuh want to go peepy where yuh would fine latrine? Nuh bush yuh would haffi go?" Miss Dassa asked.

"Is not like years ago Miss Dassa, they provide more public toilets now and the line don't reach no where near Spanish Town. That would be impossible. The road you are talking about is the toll road. People pay to use that road to get where they are going faster than the normal road," said Lorna.

"Do not listen to Miss Dassa, Grandma, she lives on a different planet," said Timothy.

"Do not be selfish Timothy. They are older people, they do not go anywhere, and therefore they are not aware of what is going on outside," Lorna said.

"Hush yuh mouth bwoy, yuh nuh kno' notin," said Miss Dassa.

"I know a lot Miss Dassa. I am going to teach you about the outside world," replied Timothy.

"Bwoy tap labba yuh mouth an' go full mi mug a coffee," said Maas Freddie. Miss Dassa stood up as straight as her back would allow. "Come Fred gitup! Yuh too glutinous! Hay Hay dem haffi go to bed soon."

They held hands and prayed for a safe trip. Timothy accompanied them home. He said, "I will bring the net for you Miss Dassa, so you can go in the net."

"De only net me want is hair net, tell Lorna carry some fi mi," said Miss Dassa.

A huge bug flew inside the house circling around Grandma Hazel. She caught the bug , spat on it and then threw it forcefully outside. Her face glowed with a smile. "Good news for tomorrow," she said.

"What was that ?" Lorna asked.

"A news bug. If it drop, that would mean bad luck, but it fly away, which mean good luck."

It was five o'clock in the morning. The loud whistling of crickets, the croaking of frogs and the noisy owls and also the sweet chirping of birds filled the air with nature's music. The fresh morning dew was the best air freshener nature could provide. Lorna started on their journey to Kingston. A few half empty buses and other motorists sped by, tooting their horns angrily at Lorna, indicating to her to dip her lights. She ignored them as she was not familiar with the narrow, deep-cornered country roads.

Lorna was nervous. Only shadows could be seen through the trees and hills. Blazing flashes of lightning showed a steep, ascending road at intervals. Rain rushed in torrents, splashing above the windows. Grandma Hazel was a bit uneasy as she was afraid of lightning. "Ah don't like traveling when rain falling at all," she said.

"It's ok Grandma, day will soon light, and the rain is going away," Lorna told her. Ten minutes later a faint ray of light was seen. Day was at hand. Suddenly the rain stopped. The traffic grew busier. By this time the buses were overloaded and passengers were standing on the steps. The mini bus drivers were racing and blocking each other, trying to get passengers. Lorna was driving as carefully as she could. She even stopped at times to allow the mini bus drivers to pass her.

When they were about half a mile from the sign post 'Welcome to Ewarton', a loud sound like a gunshot was heard. "Not at this time," said Lorna, as she slowed down.

Grandma Hazel held her chest. "A gunshot dat?" she asked. Timothy jumped from his slumber. "I have a blown tire Grandma," replied Lorna.

"Fiah?" she asked, grabbing on to her walking stick.

"No, Grandma, the car tire is punctured," Lorna answered.

"My God, a bad luck," said Grandma Hazel, displaying a disappointed look on her face. "Dis whole business mi nuh like at all, might as well we tun back," she said.

"Take it easy Grandma, we are lucky to be close to a gas station," said Lorna. She stepped out of the car. She was approached by a tall, slender rasta man. He greeted Lorna.

"Peace dawta." His teeth were ivory white. "Yuh tire flat dawta, is how far yuh coming from?" he asked.

"Rosetta," Lorna answered.

"You are a Kingstonian dawta, you going back to Kingston?" he asked.

"Yes," she answered.

"My name is Angus, but they call me Skip," he said.

"My name is Lorna, and this is my Grandmother and my son Timothy."

"Ok jus' be cool. I still no like how de beautiful queen adorn her self, but I going to help you, jus give I an' I a moment dawta. I an' I fadah want de Queens of Babylon to come before his majesty adorn in pure modest robes, an' only de king of de queen should admire de beautiful body dat Haile Selasse King of Babylon, ruler of Zion created. Yuh study I an' I dawta?" he seriously asked.

Lorna drove slowly to the gas station without responding.

"I can replace the tire, but it will take about forty-five minutes because we are not open for business yet," said another gentleman.

"Please, can you help now?" Lorna asked. "I am taking my grandmother to the embassy to get a visa."

"Embassy! You should be there overnight young lady," he said. He called another young man to fix the tire. "You have to pay a little extra if I work on it now," he said.

'Ok, how much ?" Lorna asked anxiously.

"Lady, I can't tell you until we finish," he replied.

"Oh no, I do not have much money, I need to know how much extra before you fix it," said Lorna.

"Dis expensive car, and you don't have money, a beautiful lady like you," he said.

"That does not mean I have money," she replied.

Skip came back to check on Lorna. "Grandma, you lucky if you get a visa at dis time, dem have too much rules on I an' I fadah land," he said.

Grandma Hazel replied, "Dere is rule in hell, so dere musbe rule on eart'. If dem nuh give mi, Maasa God know best."

"I agree still, Grandma. Jah say we must obey de laws of de land, for if yuh caa obey de laws of de land we will not obey de laws of Haile Selasse King of Babylon, ruler of Zion, an' therefore, yuh cannot go into de kingdom of I an' I fadah, so jus' step Grandma an' be nice to dem an' if dem give yuh de visa, yuh go an' enjoy yourself with the beautiful dawta in de land that Haile Selasse create for our enjoyment," said Skip. He touched Grandma Hazel. "Grandma de truth is, I an' I fadah want all his children to rise above de waters of Babylon, yuh nuh seet, but we are kept down by the enemies of I an' I fadah, King Haile Selasse, an' so were our ancestors. When yuh step up in de big bird dat was invented by our ancestors, is one more of Haile Selasse child rise above de waters of Babylon an' all of Zion rejoice an' give praise to de great an' mighty Haile Selasse, King of Babylon, ruler of Zion. Is de truth I an' I telling yuh Grandma, whether you believe it or not, blessed is those who believe de servant of Haile Selasse," said Skip, as he skipped backwards.

Grandma Hazel gave Skip a piercing, disturbed look. She said, "Haile Selasse is your God not mine. De God of Schedrack, Meshack an' Abendigo an' Daniel God is my God. He create you an' Helly Selasse, what eva yuh call him."

"Peace Grandma," said Skip, "hail de youth, love dawta." Lorna rewarded him. He leaped in a hopping motion like a hawk trying to touch down, shouting, "Rastafari! Rastafari!" while stroking his natty beard.

"He is nice Grandma," said Lorna.

"Yes, but 'im nuh righted. May de Lord Jesus ha mercy upon 'im poor soul, 'im musbe smoke de bush," replied Grandma Hazel. She gave Timothy an intimidating look.

Lorna continued her journey. She was driving faster than the speed limit. She ended her journey safely and was standing in line with Grandma Hazel, who was sitting in her wheelchair. She held an umbrella over Grandma Hazel, protecting her from the sun. People were complaining how far they were coming from, and how long they were waiting in the line. A tall lady whose mouth kept busy more than anyone else, stood looking at Grandma Hazel pitiably and said, "Dem people yah wicked bad, all dem olda people like she dem shoulda mek dem sidung inside insteada mek dem a wait in de bwiling sun."

A short, middle-aged man, bearing evidence of having encountered many hard knocks in life, stood looking at the tall lady and shaking his head, he said, "Woman shet yuh big mout' an' mine yuh mek dem shet de window dem. Fi mi whole life depend on de visa."

"Nuh worry," said the lady, "shut dung or nuh shut dung, nobody in dem right mine would give yuh visa fi go America wid dem deh teet wha look like a dog teet capinta put in yuh mout' an' use tar pierce dem down in yuh mout." The short man climbed on top of the rail and spat in the lady's face. She angrily picked him up with one hand, threw him over her shoulder like an evening jacket and then slammed him head first down onto the ground.

People were laughing, shouting and crowding around. Without saying a word, the security guard closed the windows and doors. More fights and quarrels broke out among the angry crowd. Grandma Hazel said, "What a disappointment, if ah did follow my mine ah would neva leave mi house, what a terrible brute dem. Dis is a sign to tell mi not to go to America."

"That is how they behave most of the time Grandma, we can try again soon," said Lorna.

"Is you alone going back," Grandma Hazel replied.

Lorna encouraged her into going back. She was the sixth in

line this time. "Next!" shouted a white, baldheaded officer. He was yawning as if he had not eaten or slept in days. He peeked through the window at Grandma Hazel. "What can I do for you pretty lady?" he asked.

"I don't know sah," she answered. She was wearing the broadest smile that her face could accommodate.

"So you would like to go to America?" the officer asked.

"Eehe, is not mi really want to go sah, is mi dawta want mi to go sah," replied Grandma Hazel.

"Are you going to America to live?" the officer asked.

"Mi not going to America to neither live nor die sah. If ah go any at all it may be only to stay a couple days, mi nat staying no where weh mi caa even go outside go warm little sun an' haffi dress like igloo wit' only mi nose outside," said Grandma Hazel .

The officer looked confused. Grandma Hazel's response seemed to trigger a smile on his bewildered face. He stamped the passport. He said, "Ok ma'am, enjoy your stay" as he handed the documents to Lorna. Grandma Hazel bowed her head sincerely.

"T'ank you sah," she said.

"Mi hearing bad, I coulda hardly hear what de bal' head man was saying," Grandma Hazel said.

"That's why you should allow me to get a hearing aid for you Grandma," replied Lorna. "You got ten years indefinite, Grandma."

"Seh wah? Ten years in deafness? About four years now mi ears giving mi trouble, is not ten years yet," she said.

"I said he gave you a ten year visa, Grandma," Lorna repeated.

"Ten years fi stay in America, ah don't even ha ten years fi live much less fi stay America," she replied.

"It means you can travel to America for ten years without renewing your visa," Lorna explained.

Timothy was busy on his cell phone calling Charmaine to give her the good news.

"Grandma, when I get back home I am going to talk to mom and then buy your ticket online early, as to get a good price," said Lorna. Grandma Hazel had no idea what the procedures were. Her eyes opened wide.

She replied, "No worry wid dat a God in heaven tall, mi nuh want notin outa dat croses line nor net, nex' t'ing it cause de plane to crash. Yuh give me de money, yuh will pay fi mi seat when I go in de plane," she said.

"Come on Grandma."

"Nuh come on mi! Before so I stay right here in my cana."

"Your corner is not safe anymore, Grandma," Lorna replied.

"No where is safe especially dat croses net line oonuh wah fi put everybody in, an' let mi tell yuh fram now, I only hope dem nuh want mi fi go on dat net to go on de plane, if nat so, an' I do go, I hope is not line nor net dem want mi go on when I want to use de toilet because I take wata pill an' need to use de toilet every minute. Every t'ing now all yuh hear bout is online or in de net," said Grandma Hazel in a quarrelsome tone.

"Don't worry Grandma, nothing like that, remember I am going with you," Lorna assured her.

Everything was well planned for Grandma Hazel's trip. She kept this a secret from the neighbourhood people except for a few friends and the church group. She was afraid the news would get to the ears of people who would break into her house.

CHAPTER
Fifteen

Lorna came home three days prior to the flight date. Grandma Hazel had every thing arranged. Her friends and the church group came to wish her a safe flight. Grandma Hazel consistently voiced her concerns about Lorna buying the ticket online, or in the net. Every one prayed for Grandma Hazel. Maas Freddie said, "Hay Hay, me nuh t'ink no body can buy ticket pan line, a only telegram run pan line."

"Maas Freddie, you are still in the cave," said Timothy.

"Nuh pay dat bwoy no mine," said Miss Dassa. She started to hum a song, then started to pray.

Miss Dassa's eyes were fixed to the ceiling. She prayed: "Dear Massa God, as dis yuh humble servant Hay Hay, about to tek her long journey to dat big place name America. God, I ask for journeying mercy for dem. An' Fadah Jesus, if dem put dem in de net I ask yuh to go in de net wit' dem for if yuh in de vessel yuh will smile at any storm dat cross dem way. O, merciful Fadah hallulah!" she shouted, as she directed them to turn in a circle three times while she repeated, "In de name of the Fadah, in de name of de Son, in de name of de Holy Ghost, tree loving spirits nava disagree, whirl without end, amen. Hallulah! Hallulah! Sonu consita! Allaba hootaaah! Allaba centa! Heeloi! Heeloi!" She held Grandma Hazel around her waist singing, "Journey man Jesus come journey wit' mi." It ended with a scream when a large cricket perched on Miss Dassa's neck. Maas Fredie lit the bottle torch. Just then a loud whistling was heard and noisy steps on the graveled walk way. It was Reverend Noblelight. "How is my flock?" he said as he shook hands. "If a when de last cock crow, I would have to come and seh a word of prayer wid my dear Mada Hazel." They stood in a circle on the verandah holding hands and prayed for a safe flight.

Miss Dassa took the bottle torch and tilted it for a brighter flame. Pastor Noblelight was praying as loud as his fluttering voice could go. They went off into a loud shouting of 'hallulah' and unintelligible tongues, which all ended in a scream. There was a loud sound of something hitting the ground but no one paid attention to it as they were deeply in the spirit. Lorna respectfully kept her eyes closed.

"Maas Freddie drop!" shouted Timothy. The spirit seemed to quickly leave everyone, as they were suddenly quiet. The flame from the torch had caught on to Maas Freddie's beard, while Miss Dassa was waving her hand in the spirit. As Timothy had no interest in what was going on, he kept his eyes open and was able to see what happened. Being frightened and without thinking, he grabbed a heavy piece of canvas that was hanging on the back of the rocking chair and he hit Maas Freddie in his face with all his strength, with the intention of putting out the flame. Maas Freddie was a frail, old man, so he fell to the floor like a fly.

Timothy and Lorna helped Maas Freddie up. He grabbed his cap and placed it on his head, while rubbing his chin. "Mi-mi-mi a'right," he said in a frightened voice. Miss Dassa asked for some butter to rub on his chin.

"No, no," said Lorna, "butter will only make it worse, do not rub it either." She immersed his chin in a dish of cold water, then applied a cream. She gave the remainder to Miss Dassa with instructions.

"Lawd, a good t'ing yuh know wha' fi do. Mi woulda haffi caa him go a hospital, den by de time de docta see 'im, 'im chin woulda rotten off."

"A good t'ing a board floor," said Grandma Hazel.

"Well, when I hear de something drop, I t'ink it was mi jacket drop off de chair back," said Pastor Noblelight. "God is good," he added.

"When mi hear de soun' mi t'ink a Parson stamp 'im foot," said Miss Dassa.

Timothy laughing as usual, said, "Maas Freddie smell like roast bird."

Maas Freddie started to laugh. "Afta yuh lick mi dung pan de floor yuh a laugh." They hugged each other, then went home.

Everyone was up early the next morning. Lorna dressed Grandma Hazel fashionably. She drove out at the same time when Maas Busha drove his noisy Land Rover out of his garage. Maas Busha had been living in the district for many years. He was highly respected, not because of his character, but because of his possessions. He was appointed Justice of the Peace, which gave him the opportunity of knowing everyone and also their business. He was well known to be very inquisitive and so earned the nick name 'District Lawyer'. He drove up beside Lorna's car, sticking his head out the window. His untidy red beard curled around his face like patches of steel-wool. His beady blue eyes peeked over his window. "Young girl, where you going so early?" he asked while scrutinizing the inside of her car. "Grandma!" he shouted. "What a way yuh look like young gal, a which young man you find gone married to?"

Grandma Hazel laughed loudly.

"Ah don't find none yet Maas Busha," she answered.

Lorna replied, "I am taking my Grandma on a trip, please give an eye on the house until we get back, not sure when."

"No problem young girl," he replied. "Anything for you. Enjoy your self Grandma and bring back a young man with you."

"All right Maas Busha," she replied. Busha looked at Lorna then drove off, sending a puff of dust and smoke in the air.

"Inqusitive retch," said Grandma Hazel. "Now de whole district will know we gone somewhere. Dat red kin retch tink mi figet seh him shot one a mi fowl. If a mosquito fly pass him place dat wicked retch shot de life outa it."

As soon as Busha got to the cross road, he stopped suddenly in front of Lorna's car, causing her to slam on her brakes in order to avoid hitting his Land Rover in the rear. A young lady was standing at the corner. She seemed to be waiting on the 'May Flower' bus. "My God!" Grandma Hazel said, "Notin but de girl dat ugly beard man si, mek him stop so sudden. A God save yuh fram hitting 'im ole noisy truck."

"You right Grandma. He is talking to her. If Busha sees a female catapillar, he stops," said Lorna.

"Any t'ing, anybody as long as a female, Maas Busha stop and pick conversation with dem," said Timothy.

"Busha is trying to get back his groove, he wants to be young again," said Lorna.

"Good God! A ole brute like dat an' 'im wife is such a nice lady," said Grandma Hazel.

"Men are never too old Grandma," Lorna replied.

Lorna and Timothy kept talking but Grandma Hazel was quiet. "Are you enjoying the ride?" Lorna asked as they waited at a stoplight. She leaned over and kissed Grandma Hazel.

"Ehe," said Grandma Hazel. "I was wondering how mi going to walk up dose steps to get in de plane."

"You will be well taken care of Grandma, no need to

worry." She patted her on her shoulder. "We are close to the airport now Grandma, I think you should drink something before we get there."

"No mam!" said Grandma Hazel. "Me not drinking one t'ing till I reach America, if I reach, for if any a yuh t'ink yuh getting mi fi go online go use toilet yuh mek a sad mistake."

"No Grandma that is impossible," said Lorna.

"Every t'ing now all mi can hear is online, online. So how dat impossible?" she asked.

"You will see Grandma," Lorna replied.

They reached the airport. Grandma Hazel looked around. "What a crowded place," she said. Timothy fetched a wheelchair for her, then helped with the luggage.

A porter walked over to where Grandma Hazel was waiting. "Which airline are you going on mam?" he asked.

Grandma Hazel looked at him with wild eyes. "Mi nat going on no line sah! I tell dem mi nuh have notin to do wit' line nor net," she angrily replied.

The gentleman wiped his face and walked away.

Along came another porter. "Where are you going honey?" he asked.

"America sah..."

Just then, Lorna came back. She replied, "We are going on Caribbean Airlines, Sir."

Grandma Hazel pointing her finger, said, "Dat man in de red cap ova dere, ask mi what line mi going on. So help me God if yuh t'ink mi going on any a oonuh crosses line."

Lorna hurriedly grabbed the wheelchair. She explained, "He means airline Grandma, the plane."

Grandma Hazel continued, "Mi an' oonuh gwine hab it out on dat plane!"

Lorna approached the door marked 'Handicap Entrance'. "Stop!" ordered Grandma Hazel, stretching out her hand. "De sign say hand de cap an' enta but mi neva worry wear no hat, wanda if ah mus tek off mi tie head give dem? But mi nuh will catch cole?" she said.

"No Grandma, people with physical limitations use this door," Lorna explained while hurriedly pushing the wheelchair in line. She ran to fetch her carry-on bag.

It was Grandma Hazel's turn. "Next in line," the officer said. "Oh, you are alone," she assumed. She walked over briskly, and pushed the wheelchair closer to the counter. "Passport ma'am," she said, stretching out her hand. Grandma Hazel did not understand a word of what she said. The officer repeated, "Passport ma'am." Grandma Hazel looked at her anxiously.

"Ah don't hear a God word what she seh," she muttered, bending forward and looking at her.

"Honey, where is your passport, is it in your purse, or did you book online?" the officer asked.

Grandma Hazel's features suddenly changed, she no doubt heard very well this time. "Mi nuh hab a God in heaven t'ing fi do wid line mam, not me," she replied angrily. Lorna came running breathlessly. "Who packed your bags?" the officer asked Grandma Hazel.

"Mi an' mi daughter mam," replied Grandma Hazel.

"Do you have any firearms, drugs, or dangerous weapons on you?" the officer asked.

Grandma Hazel's mouth opened, her face agitated. "Any bady eva hear mi trial ya," she said. "How fiah could reach in mi grip? An' when it comes to wet pan de only pan mi hab is de one what de potato pudding into. Mi hab drugs."

"Drugs!" shouted the officer.

"Oh, no, no," said Lorna.

"What yuh mean no no? Rememba mi haffi carry mi medicine what yuh buy at de drug store. I dont know how yuh forgetful so," said Grandma Hazel.

"She means drugs, her medications that the doctor ordered," Lorna explained to the officer.

"Oh, pardon me, I did not understand," said the officer. "Enjoy your stay, hon."

Grandma Hazel's cheeks widened with a smile. "T'anks mam," she replied. They made their way to the boarding area. Grandma Hazel sighed. "Mi alone could neva manage," she concluded.

The boarding announcements were made. "We are going to board the plane now Grandma," Lorna alerted her.

Grandma Hazel made a big sigh. She had a serious countenance.

"Jesus Saviour pilat me. You betta try get to de front of de line," she advised Lorna.

"It's ok Grandma," Lorna replied.

Grandma Hazel looked around anxiously. "It no ok at God tall. Look at dis big crowd a people, by de time mi get in all de seat dem gone, an' poor mi caa stan' up to hold on so dis look like a dead deal," she said.

"Shhhh," said Lorna placing her fingers over her mouth.

"Nuh shee mi!" said Grandma Hazel loudly. "You can stan' up, yuh caa expect mi fi stan' up an' mi foot dem nuh good," she said.

"Wheel chairs first," the officer announced. "Enjoy your flight," he said to Grandma Hazel.

Grandma Hazel sat in her seat next to Lorna. She felt comfortable that she had a seat and did not have to stand as she thought. She did not understand the announcements due to the accent, so she was not aware that the aircraft was already in the air. Lorna did not want to scare her. "What a long wait, by de time we reach it will be night," she said.

"No, Grandma, we are in the air already," Lorna informed her. Grandma looked at her in astonishment.

"My God," said Grandma Hazel.

"Look through the window, Grandma," said Lorna.

"Whooh," she uttered, "so how de plane go up so quiet?" Smiling contentedly, she relaxed in her seat, looking through the window momentarily.

Lunch was served. Grandma Hazel took two sips of her juice. "Drink it Grandma, you do not have to go online to use the washroom," said Lorna as she smiled. Grandma Hazel was serious, she refused to drink anymore.

"Dat is enough," she said.

The plane touched down with a jerk. Grandma looked at Lorna startled. Before she could say a word, some of the passengers were clapping and cheering.

"You are in America, Grandma," Lorna informed her.

"Seh what?" she asked surprisingly. Her face was crowned with joy.

The flight attendant helped Grandma Hazel to a wheelchair. "Did you enjoy your flight?" she asked.

"Yes mam, I enjoyed it very much," she answered. Grandma Hazel was amazed at the crowd. She waited her turn in line.

"Is this your first time here?" the customs officer asked.

"Yes sah," she answered.

"Who will you be staying with?" he asked.

"My dawta sah," she answered.

"According to your age, I know you are not going to work," said the officer, looking at Grandma Hazel as if waiting for a smart answer.

Grandma Hazel replied, "Ehe, if a when mi did name Hazel an' could work, ah would work sah, work nuh kill no body, lazy kill dem." The officer tried to identify Grandma Hazel with her picture.

"This passport has Hazel as your name. I am sorry mam but if your name has been changed, you cannot travel with this passport. You would have to change your name in the passport too."

"Change my name to what sah? Mi too old now to change name. Dis is de name my grandmother told my mother to give me, ah will neva change it sah."

"Pardon me," said the officer to Lorna. "I do not understand her accent so well. Will you repeat what she said?"

"She said she is not going to work Sir, because she is old and is not able to work anymore," replied Lorna.

"Is this her right name?" he asked. "How long are you staying ma'am?"

"Well, it depend on how t'ings going sah, it could be one day, one week or more," answered Grandma Hazel. He stamped her passport with all his strength as if trying to use up all the energy he had. "Welcome to the United States, enjoy your stay," he said, with a charming smile.

"T'ank you sah," said Grandma Hazel.

Charmaine was anxiously waiting outside. They greeted each other with hugs and kisses and made their way to the car. Charmaine opened the garage door with her remote control when they got to her house. Grandma Hazel looked around. "Den how de person who open de garage door disappear so quick?" she asked.

"I used this Mom," said Charmaine, holding up the remote control. "It is the door opener."

"Grandma, my garage door in Kingston opens just like this too. Have you forgotten?" Lorna reminded her.

"Also Maas Busha," said Timothy.

"What a change," said Grandma Hazel.

"Modern technology," said Charmaine. "That is why you need to get out of the house sometimes Mom and explore the modern world. Come Mom, you must be dying to use the washroom."

"No dalin, I wash an' press ebryt'ing before I pack them," she answered.

"Not that kind Mom, I meant the toilet. We call it washroom. And guess what Mom? You don't have to go online to use it," Charmaine said. Everyone including Grandma Hazel laughed. "I am surprised you did not wear your hat."

"Oh, I t'ink the plane woulda hab mi tossing all over an' I would lose my hat. Dat is why I tie my head tight wit de scarf until mi hab a headache," she replied. "Mi really enjoy de flight, ebryt'ing did different from what mi expec'. Whoever invent plane hab some big nerve an' ole eap a gut," said Grandma Hazel.

Timothy intervened. "Grandma, I can teach you the history of airplanes. Airplanes were invented by a gentleman named Sir George Cayel, but it was not called airplane, it was called glider. It had no engine Grandma and it could only go from a cliff to the ground."

"Dat sound like paper plane," said Grandma Hazel. Timothy's eyes grew large. "You are very smart Grandma, listen to this," he said. "Two brothers named Orville and Wilbur Wright made bicycles and discovered that bicycles that were closer to the ground were faster, so they developed the glider. They made a large two-winged kite, then read books and developed the glider, using rubber for the tail of the plane. I think in 1903, yes 1903, the Wright brothers flew a plane with only one person in it; it flew one hundred twenty feet for twelve seconds.

"Wilbur flew a second time and he went 892 feet for 59 seconds. From then on Grandma, they continued to expand on their skills. Until look at what it turned out to be today Grandma."

"Timoty yuh remember a lot, yuh not crazy all de time after all," said Grandma Hazel. "My God, an' look at de crowd of people dat was in de plane today. Fram paper to metal, fram one to a big crowd."

Everyone slept late the next morning. After many visits from friends and neighbours who came to greet Grandma Hazel, they went shopping in the big grocery stores, and visited the mall and other places of interest. Grandma Hazel was not tired of walking, she was like a young lady once more. Charmaine decided to have dinner in one of the fancy restaurants. Grandma Hazel was relaxed and was smiling from ear to ear. She ordered roast beef. A middle-aged waiter was serving. He had a strong Russian accent. He politely placed Grandma Hazel's dinner on the table. "Roast beef Babushka, yummy yummy good," he said, smiling at Grandma Hazel.

"T'ank you sah," she said.

"What dat tie tongue man call mi, baby usha?" she asked.

"No, Grandma," replied Charmaine. "He is Russian, he said 'Grandma' in Russian language."

"Afta mi nuh look like Rushan," she replied. She glanced at the roast beef then poked it with her fork. "Merciful fada, afta is nat roast beef dis." She looked at Lorna. "Dis look like ram goat liva."

"Taste it Grandma," said Charmaine, cutting a tiny piece. Grandma Hazel turned her face to the other side. "Mi nat eating it a God tall," she said as she gently pushed the plate to the side.

"Try the vegetables Grandma," said Lorna.

"Yuh nuh see seh dat nuh cook. It look like 'im steam it in de sun, a same t'ing people seh dem eat every t'ing dat hab breath ova here in America," said Grandma Hazel. "Dat meat look like wild mangoose."

Charmaine was in no way alarmed at her mom's behaviour, as she was prepared for the struggle with her adjustment to a totally new environment. She ordered fish. They were not thinking that Grandma Hazel was used to every thing well cooked, and not rare. The fish was nicely prepared and served steaming hot.

Grandma Hazel became more skeptical. She looked at the fish "Wah kind a fish dis?" she asked.

"Ooo, wait until you taste it Mom," said Charmaine who was convinced that her mother would like it. Lorna and Timothy were looking at each other. They had doubts.

"It is cat fish Mom," Charmaine told her.

Grandma Hazel's cheerful countenance changed to a distressing look. "Mi nat eating notin here, oonuh sen' mi home tomorrow," she said, holding on to her purse for security. "My God, yuh should kno' betta seh me nat eating dis, how you eat it only God kno', afta yuh nuh hab Chinese blood in yuh."

"It is not cat Grandma, it is fish," said Lorna, "everybody loves it."

"Who want fi love it, love it. Mi nuh like it nar love it," she said.

"Eat it Grandma, it will make you look younger," said Timothy. She looked at Timothy disgustingly.

"A musbe all dis foolishness yuh eat mek yuh mad so sometimes," she answered. They hurriedly ate so that they could take Grandma Hazel home to get a home-cooked meal.

"Tomorrow is Sunday mom, you will go to church. I know you do not miss out on any of your church worship," said Charmaine.

"Is Sunday already, what a way the time short here," said Grandma Hazel. "Man even shorten God time."

"It is D.S.T.," said Lorna.

"What dat mean, devil set time?" asked Grandma Hazel.

A burst of laughter was heard. "Daylight Saving Time," answered Timothy.

"Oh," she said. "Man interfere inna God business."

Charmaine stopped on the way home. "I have to get some cash," she said.

"By de time yuh get out a dat bank it will be night an' my stomach will be pack wit' gas," said Grandma Hazel.

"It will only take a minute or two, Mom." She was back in two minutes.

"That was quick. Ah neva si yuh go inside," said Grandma Hazel."

"No Mom, I used the A.T.M. outside."

"Oh all time machine," said Grandma Hazel.

"It is a computerized cash dispenser," said Charmaine.

"Yes, so people money gone in de net now, den dem tell yuh how much yuh can get out. Yes, Lawd, 666," said Grandma Hazel. "First time yuh stan' up inna long line, some people faint an' some pass to glory before dem get through. Time pass people mek unda ground vault an' keep dem money. Dis generation hab dem bread butta pan two side."

CHAPTER
Sixteen

Charmaine prepared a healthy breakfast for the family. "Mom you need to eat enough breakfast. The service is going to be longer today because it is communion Sunday."

"Mercy, is a good ting yuh talk, mi usually fas' on communion Sundays," said Gandma Hazel.

"So how about your medication Mom?" Charmaine asked.

"Ah will tek dem when mi get back fram church," she replied.

Grandma Hazel was nicely dressed in white. She was specially welcomed by Charmaine's friends, the church members and the minister. Grandma Hazel's attention was attracted by the unusual style of dressing, and the non traditional order of the service, which had no comparison to her old country home church. The minister announced the Lord's Supper. While Charmaine and Lorna were busy talking, Grandma Hazel with the help of her cane, walked to the pulpit, looking for a cushion to kneel on. She was approached by one of the ushers who was wearing the most outrageous hat. It had the shape of a circular verandah and was decorated like a bird's nest.

Grandma Hazel's cane fell to the floor. The usher felt uncomfortable bending because she was wearing a long skirt with a split up to her thighs which no doubt would expose the unexposable if she bent, so she knelt to pick up the cane. "Is there something I can help you with honey?" she politely asked. Grandma Hazel did not understand her deep American accent, so she merely smiled at the usher. Charmaine come over to her mother. "Mom, do you need to use the washroom ?" she asked.

"Washroom?" she asked. "Ah need a cushion to kneel pan."

"We do not kneel for communion Mom, we sit in our seats and they pass it around to every one." Grandma Hazel walked back to her seat with a dissapointed look on her face.

The service was over and they were on their way home. "Did you enjoy the service Mom?" Charmaine asked.

"I neva understand a God in Heaven word wha dem was saying an' how yuh parson nuh wear gown? Well, what a difference here, not even de Lord's Supper nuh sacred, good an' bad an' indifference tek it, dem serve it like it nuh mean a God in heaven t'ing. My church nuh change one bit, all de members dress in white an' fas' on communion Sundays an' yuh can tell the parson different from a some body who trying to pick pocket de offering, because my parson still wear 'im long gown an' collar. De most important t'ing we haffi kneel down an' pray till we hear a voice say 'pray no more, your sins blot out'. Because a dat most de people dem knee rough so till dem could use as washing board. Mi bring mi own cushion fi kneel pan," she concluded.

Charmaine replied, "Mom, you have to realize that we are living in a world where things are continually changing and civilization has taken over."

"Get civilized Grandma Hazel, and go with the flow," said Timothy.

"Shet fi yuh uncivilize mad mouth an' pick up yuh bible an' read it if yuh nuh have notin to do. T'ings changing fas', an' God coming fas', eheeh!" said Grandma Hazel.

"You are right Grandma," said Timothy.

Lorna and Timothy went to spend a week with Lorna's cousin Janice, who lived in Philadelphia. Charmaine worked as a nurse at the hospital close to her home. She had taken six weeks vacation and would be going back to work soon. She thought how lonely her mother would be and came up with a solution. She immediately went to talk to her about it.

"Mom, I have an idea," said Charmaine. Grandma Hazel slipped a grape into her mouth, while listening attentively to her daughter. "Mom, I will be going back to work on Monday. I am afraid you are going to be lonely so I was thinking. My friend who lives a couple blocks down the road has two girls. When I was on vacation and she was still going to work, I volunteered to watch the girls for her. Sonya pays for them at the after school center. I was thinking, since you are here she could pay you half of what she pays the center and she could leave them here with you."

Grandma Hazel, looking surprised asked, "Mi! De genkleman at de immigration place seh 'im know mi not coming here to work, dat is the only reason 'im allow mi to come here," she replied. "Mi nuh want fi break dem rule."

"You are not breaking any rule. Mom, I just want you to have a little company and at the same time you will make a little money to take home," said Charmaine.

"Eehe! If dem pay mi, is work mi working," she replied. She popped another grape in her mouth. "Nex' t'ing dem don't let mi come back here."

"Oh, so you like it here," said Charmaine.

"Sawta," replied Grandma Hazel. Her dimples appeared with a shy smile.

Charmaine hugged her. "Oh Mom, I am glad you came. You can watch the children, it will not be a problem for you."

"Alright," said Grandma Hazel. "Ah only hope dem not rude

caa dis young generation behaviour is rotten an' ah hear dat yuh caa punish pickney here or dem put yuh in prison."

"You are not allowed to spank them mother, but they are good kids, they only do kids' things. If they do anything wrong, just tell them you are going to tell me," said Charmaine.

"Eehe, mi nuh know how dat will work," replied Grandma Hazel.

"Easy," said Charmaine, patting Grandma Hazel on her back.

"They are two girls. Petra is ten years old and Pollyana is four. Petra is good with helping her little sister so you only need to supervise them. They will come at 3 p.m. and I will be home at 5 o' clock, so you will only be alone with them for two hours."

"Eehe," said Grandma Hazel. "A one year old baby will tear dis house upside down inna one minute much more two hour."

"Mom, you will enjoy them. They will keep your company."

"Yuh mean dem will company mi to mi grave," said Grandma Hazel. "Alright, let dem come. Grandma Hazel love de children, but wit' tough love."

CHAPTER
Seventeen

On Sunday evening, Sonya and her two daughters came to meet Grandma Hazel. The two girls were a bit shy. Grandma Hazel seemed to be comfortable with them. "Dem look like dem quiet," she said. Monday came and Grandma Hazel was well prepared. She was sitting by the window from 2:30 p.m., looking out anxiously for their arrival. She looked at the clock. "It is 3 o' clock, I t'ink Charmaine seh is 3 o' clock dem coming." She looked at the clock again after a little while.

"It is quarta after three, now," she said. She thought of calling Charmaine but was reluctant to use the phone. She remembered Charmaine had placed a red sticker on the button she should press whenever she needed to call her. She was just about to press the button when a car drove up in the driveway. She quickly hung up the phone and unconsciously said, "Never mind." She looked through the window, making sure it was the children, then she opened the door. A tall, white lady walked them to the door. She was wearing a broad smile on her face. Her thick, red painted lips stood out under her pointed nose. "You must be Hazel," she said.

"Yes Mam, I am Grandma Hazel, everybody call mi Grandma Hazel," she replied.

"Grandma Hazel, my name is Nancy. They are yours. Have a good evening." She quickly pushed them inside and closed the door.

"Hello my little angels," said Grandma Hazel pleasantly. Without saying a word, Pollyana and Petra pushed past Grandma Hazel and ran into the kitchen.

"I am hungry," said Pollyana.

"I want something to eat," said Petra. Their behaviour was strange to Grandma Hazel, who was a disciplinarian. She stood speechless for a while.

"What a little scamp dem, jus' push past an' neva even seh excuse." She tried to recall their names but was unable. She sternly said, "Come here bote a yuh." They came running.

"What?" Petra abruptly asked.

"From I was born," said Grandma Hazel.

"I was born too," said Pollyana, bending down and jumping up and down like a frog. "Ribbit, ribbit," she said.

Grandma Hazel sternly said, "Come to me! Bote of yuh walk back through the door." Petra saw the stern look on Grandma Hazel's face. She walked back slowly through the door and Pollyana followed her. "Now walk back inside an' don't run," said Grandma Hazel. "Now, stop an' say good evening."

"Good evening Hazel," said Pollyana, protruding her tongue at Grandma Hazel.

"Any bady eva si mi trial ya, a mi dat little retch deh stretch her tongue afta," muttered Grandma Hazel. "Listen child, Pallya, or whateva yuh name is, put a handle to mi name, mi an' yuh is not age," said Grandma Hazel, pointing her finger.

"What do you mean"? Petra nervously asked.

"What do you mean Hazel?" Pollyana asked.

"Do not call mi Hazel. Everybody call mi Grandma Hazel, so put a handle to mi name, I am older dan you," she insisted.

"Good evening Grandma Hazel," said Petra.

"You are not my Grandma," said Pollyana.

"Shut up goofy," said Petra to her sister.

"Sorry Grandma Hazel," said Petra.

"Sorry Hazel," said Pollyana.

Grandma Hazel held Pollyana's hands. "Say good evening Miss Hazel or Grandma Hazel, put a handle to mi name."

"Good evening Handle Hazel," said Pollyana, bending and grinning, making a funny face as she tried to pull her hands from Grandma Hazel's hand.

"Is your name Hazel Handle?" Petra asked.

"Call me Grandma, or Grandma Hazel. It is rude to call grown people out of dere names," she answered.

"Well, what is your real name?" Petra asked.

"Listen child, say Miss Hazel or Grandma Hazel."

"My grandma went to heaven and my other grandma lives with grandad far, far away," said Pollyana.

"My grandma closed her eyes tight and she don't want to open her eyes. Mummy says when grandma gets to heaven God will open her eyes and when we go to heaven we will see grandma. I want to go to heaven Christmas to see my grandma and get lots and lots of Christmas presents from grandma," said Pollyana. "Are you planning on going to heaven too Grandma Hazel?"

"Goofy!" shouted Petra to her sister.

"I am not goofy!" shouted Pollyana, hitting her sister

and running.

Grandma Hazel's heart was saddened. She sat hugging Pollyana and cuddling her. "Poor little t'ing," she said. "Petree! Petree!" shouted Grandma Hazel.

"Coming Grandma Hazel!" shouted Petra.

"Goofy, my sister's name is not Petree, her name is Petra," Pollyana corrected.

"Look what mi poor gal gone to," said Grandma Hazel. She shook her head and laughed.

"My name is Petra. Pet-ra," she emphasized.

"Petra or Petree, yuh know is yuh I am calling. Look on de table yuh will see cookies, milk an' grapes for bote of yuh. Wash your hands firs' an' when ever yuh need somet'ing say please."

They ran to the kitchen. "Come back here!" shouted Grandma Hazel. "What do you say?"

"Nothing Grandma Hazel. Oh, thank you Grandma Hazel," said Petra.

"Thank you Goofy," said Pollyana, laughing.

"Come here, sit right here beside mi until yuh say it de right way," said Grandma Hazel. Pollyana started to cry.

"Thank you," she said, sobbing.

"Yuh will not eat until yuh stop crying," Grandma Hazel insisted.

Petra wiped her sister's eyes. "Stop crying," she told her.

"Ok," said Pollyana, walking sideways beside her sister while glancing at Grandma Hazel.

"Say yuh grace before yuh eat," said Grandma Hazel.

"Your grace!" shouted Pollyana, stretching her hands up above her head.

"My mummy don't let us say grace," said Petra.

"Dear God," said Grandma Hazel. "Mi sure yuh say grace at school."

"We are not allowed to say grace at school. We will get punishment," said Petra. "We only used to say grace when we were living with our grandma."

They grabbed the cookies, piling them in their hands as if competing. "Put dem right back in the plate an' say your grace," Grandma Hazel repeated.

"Your grace!" shouted Pollyana.

"Not like that Goofy," said Petra as she swung her hand at her sister, spilling the cup of milk on the table and on the floor.

"Any body see mi trial," said Grandma Hazel. "It look as if a trouble mi pick up on mi head. If a so oonuh rude mi not going to able to tek care of oonuh a God tall," she said.

They did not understand a word of what she was saying. Petra rushed to clean the spill. Pollyana looked at Grandma Hazel with a saddened face. "Are you going to close your eyes tight and go to heaven like my grandma?" Pollyana asked, while she munched on her cookies.

"Mi nat allowing any a yuh to mek mi shet mi eye tight an' go a neitha heaven nor hell a God tall," answered Grandma Hazel.

"If you go to heaven, you and my grandma could go to the zoo and look at the monkeys and buy ice cream," said Pollyana, gazing at Grandma Hazel while accidentally spilling some of the milk on her clothes and the chair.

"Lawd Jesus hab mercy! It seem like a provoke de pickney dem provoke dem grandma an' sen' her poor soul a hell fi go look on monkey an' when de heat from hell tek har de poor t'ing had to buy ice cream to cool dung her self. Mi nuh t'ink mi can manage dem. My children dem neva behave like dem. Deese generation especially dis side a de whirl nuh discipline dem pickney at all," grumbled Grandma Hazel under her breath. Grandma Hazel was from the old school and such behaviour was extremely strange to her, but to the girls, she was just a mean, old lady.

Pollyana climbed onto her lap and hugged her. "Can you read me a story like my grandma did?" asked Pollyana. Pity fluttered in Grandma Hazel's heart while she tried to restrain her tears. Petra fetched a book and sat close to Grandma Hazel.

"The grapes were banging," she said. Grandma Hazel looked puzzled.

"The grapes were banging," repeated Petra in a louder tone. Grandma Hazel did not have a clue as to what she meant.

"Yuh drop dem on de floor?" she asked. "Yuh neva eat dem?"

"I ate them Grandma, that is how I know they were banging. I mean they were good," she clarified.

"Of course, mi would not give yuh if dey wasn't good."

"Banging means good and good means delicious," said Petra.

"Well, new generation, new language, new style, new world," said Grandma Hazel. She hugged them close.

They fell asleep on her lap with their heads on her bosom. She could scarcely manage to get up. She lifted their legs on to the couch and placed pillows underneath their heads. "Poor little t'ing dem, dem miss dem grandma." She wiped their hands and mouths with a wet cloth and covered them with a blanket. She sat in the rocking chair close to them watching the clock and hoping Charmaine would be home soon.

Charmaine and Lorna walked through the door at 5:05 p.m. "How were these precious little angels?"

"Eheh, you mean fallen angels?" Grandma Hazel asked.

"Did they give you a hard time mother?"

"A God sorry fi mi an' put dem to sleep, otherwise I woulda gone a heaven gone look at monkey an' buy ice cream," replied Grandma Hazel. "Poor little t'ing dem, so dem grandma died fi true?"

Lorna took a seat close to Grandma Hazel. She explained, "Their grandmother used to take good care of them, but she passed away unexpectedly."

"Stroke nuh," Grandma Hazel assumed.

"No, she was hit by a drunk driver while crossing the street. She was going to shop for Christmas gifts for the family."

"Poor t'ing. Oh God, dat drunkin' retch," said Grandma Hazel in a sad voice. "Dem rude, but mi will try mi bess to help out wid dem for de little time I'm here. By de way, dem punish de children if dem pray at school?" asked Grandma Hazel.

"Only the private schools allow prayers in their schools," replied Charmaine. "Mom, I am happy you arc here and you are willing to help with the girls. Maybe you will help their psychological needs that they have developed since the death of their grandma."

As time went by, Grandma Hazel got attached to them and they also to her. Very soon they started to call her 'Grandma Hanna' like their real grandmother. She tried to fit in by doing most of the fun things that their real grandmother used to do with them. She made beautiful outfits and blankets for them, she trained them and showed love and affection. They came to realize that she was not a mean old lady after all.

Grandma Hazel became more comfortable and was even feeling and looking young again. She was out shopping with her daughter up to 10:00 p.m., while in Jamaica she retired to bed as early as 7:00 p.m., except on church nights. She enjoyed outings with the church group and going bowling, even scoring higher than some of the young people.

Lorna and Timothy came back from Philadelphia and prepared for their flight back to Jamaica. Surprisingly, Grandma Hazel wanted to stay for a longer time. Lorna and Timothy travelled home, leaving Grandma Hazel to enjoy herself some more.

CHAPTER
Eighteen

Charmaine took a week off from work to travel home with her mother. Grandma Hazel was admired and loved by Charmaine's friends, neighbours and church group, so she collected many gifts. Grandma Hazel shopped for everyone she knew, causing her daughter to think that she would need her own private jet to enable her to take all her baggage home. Grandma Hazel smiled. She said, "Ah had de wrong idea bout America, mi like it here, everyone is nice."

"So mother, would you think of living here?" Charmaine asked.

She sat up straight and replied, "Mi really like it here, but ah don't want to live here. Ah will keep on traveling as long as ah can."

It was a very bright and sunny day with mild humidity, which made the atmosphere great for travelling. Charmaine and her mother were on their way to the airport. "Next in line!" shouted the immigration officer who looked as if he had never smiled from the day he was born.

"Did you enjoy your stay?" the officer asked.

"Yes sah," answered Grandma Hazel.

"Good for you," he said as he stamped her passport.

Grandma Hazel was more relaxed on the flight this time. They got home safely and although tired from traveling, she insisted on staying up, making sure everything was as she had left them. Miss Dassa and Maas Freddie were the first to visit the following day.

Miss Dassa stood at the door looking and smiling from one ear to the other. She greeted Lorna with a hug and a loud kiss. Hugging Grandma Hazel, she said, "Lawd Hay Hay, what a way yuh tun yung gal, yuh even put an lily flesh ova yuh bone, yuh look good ma."

Grandma Hazel was excited to see her friends. "Come in mi dear mam," she said. They sat down.

Maas Freddie asked, "Den Hay Hay. Yuh like America?"

"To tell yuh de truth Maas Freddie, mi so glad mi did go. Mi enjoy miself an' to mi surprise most a wha people seh bout America is not true at all. Ah get to sit outside ebry day."

Miss Dassa opened her mouth wide. "Seh wha Hay Hay, den how dem seh people unda lock an' key day an' night?"

"Not like dat," Grandma Hazel explained. "I sit by de pool, I sit on de verandah, I mean porch as dem call it ova dere an' sew. Mi go to de store dem, an' buy t'ings. De store dem big so till is wheel chair Charmaine let mi use to get around. Den dem hab some fancy buggy what people can use if dem caa walk well, but mi woulda neva use dem fah dem hab steering wheel an' mi fraid mi may go lick dung people."

"Eh mi dear ma!" replied Miss Dassa.

Grandma Hazel continued, "Mi go bowling an score higher dan de young people dem."

Age had robbed Maas Freddie of his ability to hear well.

He asked, "Wah kina bowl yuh scowa, mek yuh scowa more dan dem? Afta dem young people nuh kno notin bout scowa bowl, dem only kno' fi eat outa it."

"Bowling Maas Freddie, is a game where you pick up a big, tough, heavy ball wid tree hole in it, yuh put yuh tree fingas in de tree hole dem an' roll de ball on a track an' try knock dung all de pin dem," Grandma Hazel explained.

"Pin?" Maas Freddie asked.

"Yes fool, safety pin like wha pin up yuh trouses waise," said Miss Dassa.

"Oh! Den dat nuh easy, any baby coulda win dat," said Maas Freddie.

Grandma Hazel said, "No, is not latch pin, is wooden pins in a group a nine or ten. Each pin a almos' five inch wide an' fifteen inch tall."

"Yuh learn a whole heap since yuh go way. Nex' time mi haffi come wid yuh," said Maas Freddie.

"Shet yuh mout! Yuh woulda haffi go a night when eh dark so no bady nuh see yuh, an' yuh woulda sleep pass yuh stap," Miss Dassa said.

Maas Freddie replied, "All mi woulda do a carry mi bicycle wid mi an' ride back to where mi going. Den Hay Hay, a true seh de plane mek up so much nise dat when people reach a dem stop dem haffi hit de side a de plane hard hard so de pilat ca hear because 'im haffi shet up inna one cubby hole to prevent de breeze fram blow him out?"

"No man, notin like dat. Mi neva wear mi hat because ah t'ink de breeze on de plane woulda ha mi tossing all ova, but to mi surprise, ah neva even feel a breeze. If Lorna neva tell mi seh de plane was up in de sky, mi woulda neva kno'."

"Den, yuh get any seat?" Maas Freddie asked.

"Yes man, it was so much people dat ah was hurrying Lorna to get to de front a de line so dat ah would get a seat. But notin like dat," replied Grandma Hazel.

"So tell me sometin, Hay Hay, yuh neva haffi go an' line nor in de net to use de latrine?" Miss Dassa asked.

"When ah was goin mi dear ma, ah neva drink a sip of wata caa mi did fraid mi woulda haffi go online to use de toilet or wash room, but notin like dat, for when we comin' back mi use de toilet an' it was neda on de line nor in de net. Hope dem will neva go online fi now because mi woulda like to go back to America as long as God spare mi life," said Grandma Hazel.

"Lawd Hay Hay we way behine time," said Miss Dassa.

"Is nat jus' we," replied Grandma Hazel. "Would yuh believe dat dere was a woman on de plane who was born, in America, an' she was asking har son if she haffi stan' up an' hole on. Her son favor like him shame like a dog, 'im cova her mout' quick an' wispa in her ears. Den she talk so loud people hear an' was laughing afta her. Plenty American nuh kno what inside a one plane look like," said Grandma Hazel.

"Dats a burden shame," said Miss Dassa.

Charmaine woke up and heard the conversation. "Nothing wrong with that," she said. "Some of them are afraid to fly. Or have no reason to fly. They can drive to other states or some of them can't afford the money."

"Seh wah! Mi hear dat ebry bady in America rich," said Maas Freddie, his eyes bulging like a frightened patoo.

"No, there are very poor people in America. Some are even homeless, living on the streets, and some living in old shacks just like some people in other countries," Charmaine explained.

"Is true," Grandma Hazel agreed. "Mi did surprise fi kno'. Ebry t'ing is so different dere. Mi go church wid Charmaine. De people dem nice, but when dem serve de Lord Suppa, dem don't do it sacred like how we do it inna fi wi church here. Dem give fram de cradle to de grave, who undastan', an' who nuh undastand. Worthy an' unworthy, ungodly an godly, even one man ah see run in sweating like 'im jus' rob somebody an' trying to escape an' dem serve 'im communion too." She paused and shook her head before continuing. "Our parson wear 'im long white or black gown an' 'im white collar, even doa sometime we nuh kno' if is white or yellow, but 'im wear it. De church where Charmaine go, yuh don't kno' 'im de parson, fram de criminal coming fi repentance.

"Mi rememba when mi go Kingston, mi an' Lorna go night service. We go late, ah went to dis man an' ask 'im to pray for my arthritis joint, de man look at mi an' seh, 'Grandma, count yuh blessing, mi looking for de parson to pray fi mi bruk ankle an' mi bruk arm.' But more dan dat, mi couldn't see outa mi lef' eye fi days."

Maas Freddie asked, "Wha happen, yuh ketch up cole?"

"No sah, nuh de hat dem wha' de women dem wear to church, dem hab upstairs, dung stairs an' a whole heap a antenna sticking out, nuh one a de antenna fram de parson wife hat stick mi inna mi eye when she did a hug mi. Any way, so ah was rubbing mi eye an' she seh, 'Don't cry honey what eva de problem is, God will fix it.' Den her lip dem red like when we rub annatto inna wata to make frittas."

"Ah only hope de good Lord fix har hat fi har," Miss Dassa replied. "Hay Hay every t'ing change. Yuh memba we cassava hat, all we do is buy piece a ribban an' tie roun' it an' buy piece a net put ova it. Den de net cova we face an' de cremoline well starch dat some a we haffi walk sideways to get trough de door. Dem time deh we well dress."

Maas Freddie said, "Fi mi li piece a red cap, mi jus' fole it up an' push it in mi back pocket, when de spirit tek mi so man it drop out an' dem trample it to pure tread."

Miss Dassa hissed her gum. She asked, "Which spirit tek you?" She looked him up and down and said, "A musbe de spirit fram de Captain Morgan white rum what yuh use fi drink an drain de bottle before yuh go inna de church, yuh an' dem people uppa top road."

"Dem time deh mi full a de spirit," said Maas Freddie.

"Yes, yuh full till yuh vomit an' tun foola prechi," said Miss Dassa, cutting her eyes.

Charmaine tried to explain the changes that had taken place, but Grandma Hazel continued to talk about all that she thought was strange. She continued, "De nex' t'ing I notice, it look like nobody nuh bawn wit' short hair no more. Almost ebry bady wit' dis long head a hair all de way to dem waise, even de little baby dem. I wanda how dem grow hair so fas', if dem start bawn wit' whole heap a hair now since every t'ing change. Some a dem pile it up on dem head like London Bridge, an' all who fa hair was short, jus' start grow fas' like crab grass."

"Nuh musa wax dem wax it like rasta," said Maas Fredie. Miss Dassa hissed her gum dismissively. "Yuh always talk fooliness. A nuh God given hair dem ha, a somet'ing dem call, am, am, oh, distincton, dem put on tap a dem hair."

"Oh, an' it look so real," said Grandma Hazel.

"No ma mi nuh t'ink so, it musbe wig," said Maas Freddie.

"No," said Grandma Hazel.

"Ask Charmin," said Miss Dasssa, "Charmin, what dem call de style what people put on dem hair nowadays?"

"Style?" asked Charmaine.

"Yes, someting like distinction."

"Oh, do you mean extension?" Charmaine asked.

"Das right, das what ah mean," said Miss Dassa.

"My God, so man start mek hair now?" Grandma Hazel asked.

"Mom, some is synthetic and some is real human hair," Charmaine replied.

"Sen' stick an' wha?" Miss Dassa asked.

"Some is real and some is not real," said Charmaine.

"De only t'ing man cah do a blow breat'," said Maas Freddie.

Grandma Hazel clapped her hands and said, "Well when ah was in Kingston, right at de hospital where Lorna have her baby, ah si a man drop an' dem call de ambulance. De man in de blue uniform ben dung ova him an' seh 'im nat breading. An' ah si two a dem kneel ova de dead man. One a dem kneeding 'im ches' wid 'im two hand dem an' de oda one blow in 'im mout', an' to mi surprise, de man start move 'im finga an open 'im eye, but ah believe de man was a preten' or maybe drunk for man will neva be able to blow breat'; cares nat how dem try."

"Den how man go to de moon?" Maas Freddie asked.

"Dem nuh go to no moon, de moon come to dem, don't yuh si de moon come out every night. Rain or nuh rain, if de whole moon caa come even half come an' sometime a quarta come , but it come," said Miss Dassa.

Charmaine sat close to Miss Dassa. Miss Dassa sniffed. "What a way yuh smell sweet," she said.

"Thank you," said Charmaine, smiling. "Ok, I will explain something to you. What you saw the man doing to the other man who was lying on the ground is called cardiopulmonary resuscitation. The man had a heart attack and they had to do that to get his heart working again."

Grandma Hazel gave a doubtful look. She said, "I neva see no car pullin no station, dat is not what mi talking bout a God tall."

"Mom, I said car-dio-pul-mon-ary re-su-sci-tat-ion," Charmaine emphasized.

"Somet'ing wrong wid yuh ears, yuh expose to too much cole in America," said Grandma Hazel.

"Never mind Mom," said Charmaine. "I will explain it to you again later."

"De latest t'ing now is when dem find out dem wrong, all yuh ca hear is, never mine, never mine," said Grandma Hazel. "Firs' time when people drop dung, all dem do is put ammonia at dem nose, an' eida dem jump up or dem stiff dead. Dem neva know if a heart attack or duppy attack an' nuh bady nuh pull no cart, or whateva Charmaine seh it name," said Grandma Hazel. "De nex' t'ing I can hardly believe. Yuh kno' dat firs' time if a woman barrin, she stay barrin, now mi hear seh de docta dem tek baby outa man, an' put inna woman."

"How docta fi tek baby outa man an' man caa ha baby?" Maas Fredie asked.

"Yuh fool fool sah, a dat why mi read book," Miss Dassa firmly said. "De something what de docta tek out af de man an' put in de woman name sprout, dat is what de docta tek outa de man an' put in de woman!"

"Sperm, not sprout," said Charmaine.

"Dem change de name of everyting, all we olda head soon haffi stap talk," said Maas Freddie.

"No, we jus' need to go out sometimes an' get in de light," said Grandma Hazel.

"A true Hay Hay," said Miss Dassa.

"Yes mi dear ma, since mi start go to Kingston an' America, it surprise mi to si how every t'ing change up. It mek all de ola head dem feel laas," said Grandma Hazel.

"Den Hay Hay it gwine get worsa when we haffi do everyt'ing pan de line an' in de net," Miss Dassa said and laughed. "De only t'ing poor me able to do pan line a heng clothes, an' when it come to de net, me only know to wear it pan mi head."

"An' even de ole people dem no badda wid hair net no more," said Grandma Hazel.

"A true ma, all a dem a wear de distinction, oh, ex, ex, what eva Charmin seh it name," said Miss Dassa.

"Maybe by dat time we will be gone to our maka," said Grandma Hazel.

"By dem time deh mi kick de bucket lang time," said Maas Freddie.

"Fred yuh no hab a t'ing fi worry bout, de only t'ing yuh eva do good a snore, yet yuh eye dem still half open," said Miss Dassa.

Maas Freddie opened his beady eyes as wide as they could and said, "A lie yuh a tell, yuh nuh si mi big son."

"Big son!" Miss Dassa exclaimed. "Yuh nuh see seh a big jacket. De bwoy kin red like fi Busha an bote 'im muma an fi yuh family black like chalk coal."

"Good t'ing mi neva mine a wha colla egg mi wife hatch, far a 'im a tek care a we now," said Maas Freddie. They had a big laugh, then lit the bottle torch to see their way home.

"Surprise! Welcome to modern invention," said Charmaine as she handed them a rechargeable flashlight. "This means your beard will not catch a fire anymore."

"Lawd, yuh a lighten we up," said Maas Freddie.

"Gimmie!" said Miss Dassa, "yuh soon drop eh, t'anks Miss Charmin."

Grandma Hazel continued travelling to Kingston and Florida. She became more and more comfortable with travelling. She interacted with the young people so much that she had changed and got used to some of the things she once dreaded, like electricity and appliances.

CHAPTER
Nineteen

Grandma Hazel celebrated her ninety-seventh birthday. She was still moving around and had the features of a seventy-year old. Her health was slowly deteriorating but she kept as active as she could. Grandma Hazel became sick and needed to go to the hospital miles away from home. This was her first time in a hospital. Grandma Hazel maintained her strong spirit, and she recovered and went to stay with Lorna for a while.

Grandma Hazel became homesick, so she went back to her own home. "What a relief," she said, as she walked through the door. "Notin like yuh owna home." After much persuasion from Lorna and Charmaine, she agreed to have someone stay with her. Grandma Hazel got sick several times, and she was hospitalized a second time. Charmaine came home to be with her. Timothy graduated from university with a degree in Physical Therapy and was able to help Grandma Hazel with therapy.

Grandma Hazel recuperated and was home once more. Charmaine hired a caregiver for her mother, but as time went by, Grandma Hazel's care became overwhelming for her caregiver, so Charmaine had to make different arrangements. One day she decided to have a talk with her mother. With some doubt in her mind, she said, "Mother, I was thinking. Since I am a nurse and I'm familiar with your care, also considering your present needs, I think it would be in both of our best interest that I take you home with me." Charmaine hugged her. "What do you think?"

Grandma Hazel held her breath for a moment, then let out a deep, distressing sigh. She replied, "Ah don't t'ink mi able to tek anedda trip to America as much as mi woulda like fi go." Her face was saddened. "Ah want to spend mi last days here."

There was a moment of silence and then Charmaine explained, "There is no one here to give you the care you need, Mother. You can still travel back if things work out better for you. I will travel with you."

Grandma smiled pleasingly. "Alright, ah t'ink ah will enjoy anedda trip to Florida, may be de last one," she said.

She made sure everything she needed was packed and then she was in America with her daughter once more. She was given the best care possible. She was still sitting on the porch doing her needle work as usual and still enjoyed going to church with her daughter, whenever she could. Though encouraged to stay, Grandma Hazel was afraid her house would be burglarized. She also missed her church and friends, though most of them had passed away.

Charmaine and her mother were having breakfast and Charmaine looked at the calender. "Mother," she said, "you only have two weeks before your travel date."

"My God, de time fly fas'," Grandma Hazel said as she stopped eating, looking surprised.

"Well we can change your flight if you would like to stay longer," said Charmaine.

Grandma Hazel cleared her throat.

"I hear dat when people stay longa dem cancel dem visa," she said.

"No Mom, only people whom they assume are working here illegally who stay in the country longer than they are suppose to."

"Well, ah will stay one more mont', only hope dem nuh break into de house," she said.

"Mom, remember Maas Busha is watching, and Lorna or Timothy will go down and check," Charmaine reassured her.

Grandma Hazel was enjoying her time, but kept having nightmares about her house being burglarized. Her time was up and she was ready for her trip home. Charmaine accompanied her. There was shocking news that caused Grandma Hazel to be overwhelmingly unhappy. Maas Freddie had passed away two days prior to her returning home. She was comforted by the fact that she had the opportunity of attending his funeral to pay her last respects.

Miss Dassa had gotten progressively weak and was gravely depressed from the death of her husband. She was forced to live with her neice in Mandeville since she had no children of her own. Grandma Hazel missed her very much. Lorna came home to stay with her for the long summer holiday. She was teaching at a Catholic high school, and had made arrangements to be transferred to another branch in the country, enabling her to over see and help with the care of her grandmother. Lorna drove to Mandeville twice per month, taking Grandma Hazel to visit Miss Dassa.

Miss Dassa passed away from a massive heart attack shortly after moving in with her neice. Unfortunately, Grandma Hazel could not attend her funeral since she was sick and confined to bed at the time, but Lorna and Timothy attended. Grandma Hazel was depressed. Her health was deteriorating and she had no interest in the things she once loved to do. Soon she became so ill she had to be visited regularly at home by her doctor.

One morning as Charmaine got home from work, the phone rang. It was bad news. Her mother had gotten worse. The doctor said she would not make it to the weekend due to congestive cardiac failure, and kidney failure. Charmaine was saddened. "Hang in there Mom, do not go anywhere, I will be there soon," said Charmaine, her voice thickened with suppressed sobs.

"Yuh haffi come now," said Grandma Hazel, her voice low and weak.

"Hello! Hello!" Wonda, the caregiver, took the phone. "You have to come now," she said.

"Tell Lorna to take her to the hospital until I get there," Charmaine told her. Timothy and Lorna were unable to get an ambulance, and had to pick her up.

It was night time, there were miles of traffic moving bumper to bumper, or not moving at all. Angry drivers were tooting their horns. Some were cursing and swearing while others came out of their vehicles and started a few fights. Grandma Hazel was groaning painfully.

"What's going on?" Timothy asked, as a policeman approached the vehicle.

"Accident miles away boss," the young officer replied. He looked confused.

"My grandmother is very sick, she is dying, and we are trying to get her to the hospital, can you let us through please?" Lorna pleaded.

"There is nothing I can do now because it's more than one accident and traffic back up away and is me alone," said the policeman.

"She is having heart failure, officer please, please see what you can do," said Lorna. The officer stepped out in the road. He blew his whistle.

"Driver see if you can squeeze on the shoulder of the road and cut through some of the traffic," the officer instructed as he blew his whistle and directed Timothy where to go. There was an outburst by the angry crowd of people. Some were helping the officer to direct the traffic. One angry driver turned his vehicle crossways the road as soon as Timothy tried to get through. "Man why you do that? We have my great grandmother here, she has heart failure, and we are trying to get her to the hospital, she is dying!" said Timothy.

"Yuh too lie, yuh gwine wait like all a we," he said.

Lorna said, "Look, here she is, she is my grandmother and we are trying to save her life. You need to move your car and let us through."

The angry, ignorant man did not look. He laughed instead. Pointing his finger, he said, "Yuh se da ambulance deh, one woman in deh a dead. She even have nurse in deh an' a long time it nuh move from weh it sidung. Oonuh lie to blouse an' skirt, a because oonuh want fi go tru." He walked away, leaving his vehicle crossway the road.

Timothy and Lorna were very angry. "How can one policeman manage all this traffic?" Lorna asked as she jumped out of the vehicle and started to direct Timothy to squeeze by.

It was impossible. There was no where to detour. After hours of waiting and driving bumper to bumper, Grandma Hazel got to the hospital alive, but looked as if she was taking her last breath. She was treated in the ER and later admitted to the private wing. Every procedure was strange to her and her expression of agony was evident. As Grandma Hazel was placed in her bed, she said, "My God what a suffering pan de road, t'ank God I mek it alive, what a change. People getting more an' more selfish. But de word of God say when de end is near, people will be lovers of dem self." The medication took effect and she fell into a deep sleep.

Lorna and Charmaine stayed at the hospital with her.

Charmaine had arrived on a late flight and came straight to the hospital. Grandma Hazel refused to adhere to her sodium free diet and ate poorly, limiting her recovery. She had many visitors whom she interacted with. She was sleeping earlier than usual and the nurse came in to administer her medication. "Grandma went to sleep earlier tonight, she is tired from having so many visitors," the nurse commented.

Charmaine was up early. The sun was shining through the window. She was already dressed and was about to give her mother her morning bath, but she could not be awakened. "Give her another hour, she must be overly tired," Lorna suggested. Two hours passed and she was still asleep. Charmaine was anxious and afraid.

The doctor came in. "Prepare for the worse, her lab results are not good. She has a very bad heart." He looked at Charmaine, whose eyes were filled with tears and said, "Your mom is a strong lady, so be strong." Grandma Hazel was unresponsive to even painful stimuli. The family was notified and they arrived quickly.

Pastor Noblelight was also notified. He traveled from the little village and was accompanied by a group of church members. He was dressed in a suit that fit as if he'd had it since he was in his twenties though he was now in his late eighties. The sleeves were extraordinarily short, the colour was badly faded and looked like if he took a deep breath all the buttons would fall off. He was carrying an attaché case that was looking as sad as he was. One could have guessed that Noah must have used it to safekeep the documents in the ark.

His wire-framed spectacles was riding on his nose, which had no bridge, so he could not look left nor right without holding it from falling. "My name is Reverend Noblelight, and these are my flock. We are here to say goodbye to our dear Mother Hazel," he said.

The nurse asked: "You are here to say good what?"

"God spoke to me, on our way here," he said. "Hurry, I am only lending you a little more breath until you get dere, but you see, God speaks in parables, so he means our dear sister, Mother Hazel."

"Ok Sir, go ahead to room 212 but only one at a time," the nurse instructed.

"Nurse, the good book say, where two or tree meet touching anything concerning Him God, He will be dere to bless. God neva say where one meet, and when we pray, togeda, it more powaful nurse," said Pastor Noblelight.

"Amen! Amen! Hallelujah!" shouted one of the ladies, stamping her feet and bending as if she urgently needed to use the washroom.

A ward assistant was passing by, she had no idea what was going on. "The toilet is just around the corner in the hallway behind you lady. You going to peepy up your self like yuh a pickney?" she asked.

"Ok Sir, go ahead, but you cannot be long," said the nurse. "Dem look like dem come fi tek de woman breath away," the nurse grumbled under her breath. "Bout yuh name Revrend Nobelight."

"'Im musbe mean Revrend Crazy," said another nurse.

"Dillusion of grandur," a student nurse said, "Am I right, I have to catch up on my psychology practice."

The lady kept on stomping her feet in a right, left motion. "Lady mi jus' done clean de floor, mine yuh wet up yuh self. The toilet is right behind you. Like how yuh see me tiad ya," the cleaning lady said, hissing her teeth.

The group started out quietly, but graduated to loud clapping and shouting. The scripture the pastor read was as if he was at the grave side. He ended by saying, "God, please receive her dear soul." The nurse closed the door quickly.

"My God," she said. "The other patients will soon be running out of here thinking there is a burial plot in the building." Charmaine was not annoyed by the noise as she was hoping her mother would be awakened, but she slept on. Pastor Noblelight said, "Mother Hazel opened her eyes as soon as I called her name." He was the only one from the group who saw.

"Nurse! Nurse! Nurse!" shouted a few voices as they came running breathlessly to the nurses' station screaming and crying. "Come quick nurse!"

"No need to be frightened, we were expecting this to happen. Honey, remember she is ninety-eight years old. I know you will miss her, and we miss her too," said the nurse patting the lady on her shoulder. She went into the room. "But she is in a — oh my God!" shouted the nurse as she called for help. "Code Blue! Code Blue!"

Pastor Noblelight was on the floor and was pronounced dead after several attempts of cardiopulmonary resuscitation. It was one of the most devastating situations that had taken place in the hospital that afternoon. Almost everyone's attention was attracted by Pastor Noblelight's tragedy. Grandma Hazel kept on sleeping throughout the excitement.

A loud voice was heard calling, "Eartquake! Eartquake! Wha mek yuh a walk so fas' like yuh a run go ketch t'ief?"

"Yuh nuh hear wha happen ova de private wing?" Earthquake replied.

"Mi nuh hear notin boss, a ova outpatient mi jus' a come from."

"Yuh memba de little funny looking man wha jus' pass we, an' 'im have on one bad colour white calla an' some adda people was wit him, look like dem jus' escape from Bellevue? Well, dem seh 'im a parson an' 'im go pray fi one sick woman an' 'im drop dead an' lef' de woman still a sleep boss," Earthquake said.

"Kiss mi neck, yuh sure yuh hear good? A wha yuh really a seh, someting go so fi true boss?" the porter asked.

"An' mi hear seh a far out in de country dem come from all de way up here boss," Earthquake added.

"Wait fi mi, mek mi go drop dis a de pharmacy," said the porter who walked off as fast as he could go. "Eartquake! Eartquake! A yuh a de undataka? Wait fi mi boss!"

Charmaine's friend Sonya and her daughters Pollyanna and Petra came to see Grandma Hazel and to give moral support to Charmaine. Petra was now a teenager. She walked through the door, remembering Grandma Hazel calling her "Petree" and her little sister saying "Handle Hazel". Petra looked at Grandma Hazel. "Wake up Handle Hazel! It's Petree," she said, squeezing Grandma Hazel's great toe.

Grandma Hazel opened her eyes and took a deep breath. "Mom! Mom!" Charmaine screamed, hugging and kissing her mother. Grandma Hazel's heart rate elevated, then gradually dropped near to normal. She yawned like a hungry bird.

On entering the room, the nurse asked, "What, she is gone?"

"She is awake! Strange things are happening in this room," said a staff member. The news spread fast. Soon the room was filled with staff and visitors, and it was difficult to keep people out. Some were crowding the hallway stretching their necks in. The nurse closed the door. Earthquake and the porter had just gotten to the wing and saw the crowd and heard what had happened. Earthquake looked at the porter and the porter looked at Earthquake, their eyes bulging from their sockets. "So tell mi somet'ing to back foot," Earthquake said. "De woman wake up same as de parson man dead? A wah kina... lisen to dis boss, mi jus' hear one a de relative seh de woman husband dead long time, yuh remba de big write up inna de news paper years ago boss? Seh 'Dead Man Move In Casket, Crowd Scattered'?"

"Oh, yes, yes boss, mi memba boss. A de same day Goose Neck hia mi an' mi start work in here boss, a dat how mi memba, da day deh, every body run go buy newspaper boss."

Goose Neck was the nick name given to the recruiting officer whose legal name was Gerald Righthorne. He was called Goose Neck because of his extraordinary tall neck. "Aright, listen dis boss, an' tell mi if mi wrong. Dem seh a did fi har husban move inna de casket so a nuh notin but de dead man want him wife fi join him an' de parson man fine himself all de way ya come bout him a pray fi de woman live longa an' de dead husban 'im nuh like it bass so de duppy lick dung de parson man."

"Yuh have a salid pint deh oonuh Eartquake," the porter replied.

"Hear mi boss, yuh can stay, but yuh see mi, mi gone to back foot, nex' t'ing me go drop dead to."

"A true boss, an' me have my little youth dem fi tek care of."

"Look ya boss, life hard, but eh sweet still, yuh nuh check," said Earthquake as he and the porter made their way out of the wing as fast as they could back to their work areas, spreading the news all around.

Petra asked Grandma Hazel, "Who am I?"

"Petra," she replied.

"Who is this?" Petra asked, touching her sister.

"Pollyanna," Grandma Hazel replied. "Weh mi deh? Mi neva rememba ah was in America. Ah musbe was sleeping," said Grandma Hazel.

Charmaine replied, "No Mom, you are in Jamaica. They came all the way here to see you."

She looked around surprised. "My God," she said, her smile followed by a grimace from the pain when she tried to move her leg. The doctor made his visit and was on his way out. "We are very excited, but we need to take it easy for now," said Dr. Singualli.

Grandma Hazel was discharged in four days. Charmaine stayed for a month, making sure all was well. She took her mother to America with her. It was a constant struggle for her to adjust to the rapid changes around her and how the advances in technology were really designed to make life easier for everyone.

To the end, she maintained her unique, strong-willed character and remained a firm disciplinarian.

Patois Defined

A

Afta - after

Afta birt - after birth (placenta)

A fi mi - it is mine

Anada/anedda - another

Ano - is not

A ow - I hope

B

Baan - born

Babylon - nickname for police; a Rasta word for the police and the corrupt system

Bada - worry

Bade - bath

Badaration - trouble

Bady - body

Bat-bat - behine, bottom or backside

Battam - bottom

Bawl - cry

Beas - nickname for police

Bahine - behind

Bline - blind

Bote - both

Bout - about

Bruk - broke, broken, break

Bud - bird

Bun - burn, to get cheated on; also burn, kill, and to smoke

Butta - butter

Bwiling - boiling

Bwoy - Boy

C

Caa - cannot

Calla - collar

Cana - corner

Chat - talk

Cho - expression of disgust or frustration

Cola - color

Coo - look

Cova - cover

Cus - curse

Cuss-cuss - shouting fight with bad words

Cut yeye - cutting your eye at someone by turning your eyes the other way

Cuyah - look here

D

Dalin - darling

Docta - doctor

Dan - than

Dat - that

Dawta - daughter; woman

Debble - devil

Deh - there also to ask where something is

Dere - their

Dese - these

De - the

Dis - this

Dose - those

Draws - underwear

Driva - driver

Dung - down

Duppy - ghost; spirit

E

Ears ole - years old

Eben - even

Ebry - every

Ehe - yes

Eida - either

Ena - in

Eye wata - tears

F

Fa - for

Fadah - father

Fah - for

Falla - follow

Fambly - family

Fambly way - pregnant

Fashan - fashion

Fass - fast; rude or nosey

Fava - favour; looks like; resembles

Fawud - forward

Fedda - feather

Fiah - fire

Figat - forget

Figet - forget

Finga - finger

Fi mi, fi she, fi yuh, fi im -
     mine; hers; yours; his;
     Shows possession

Firs - first

Fraid - afraid

Fram - from; since

Fren - friend

G

Gaan - gone

Galang - go along

Gimme - give me

Girout - go away

Git up - get up

Govament - government

Grang-grang - fine dry
     branches

Grung - ground

Gwaan - go

Gweh - go away

Gwine - going

H

Ha/Hab - have

Haffi - have to

Han - hand

Handkechiv - handkerchief

Head wata - amniotic fluid

Heng - hang

Hia - hire

Higgla - a street vendor

Hole - hold; old

Husban - husband

I

Iah - rastafarian

Ima - he is

Inna - in; into

In deh - in there

Inspecta - inspector

J

Ja, Jamdown, Jam-dung -
     Jamaica

Jinc   join

K

Kakah - feces

Ketch - catch

Kina - kind of

Kine - kind

Kin -   skin

Kip - keep

Kno - know

L

Laas - last, lose or lost

Labba-labba - talks a lot; talking too much

Lan - land

Lawd a massy - Lord have mercy

Lef - leave, left, passed

Letta - letter

Lick - hit

Lick dung people - knock people down

Li/Lilly - little, tiny

Lissen - listen

M

Maas - mister

Mad - out of mind; without sound mind

Madhouse - mental institution

Maga - skinny; slender

Mawin - morning

Mannas - manners

Maskitta - mosquito

Matta - matter

Mek - let; make

Memba - member; remember

Mi - me, I, mine

Minista - minister

Mout - mouth

Mose - most

Muma/mudda - mother

Munt - month

Mussa - must have

Musbe - must be

Muss - must

Mussi - must be

N

Nappy - diaper

Neba - never

Neda - another

Nex - next

Notin - nothing

Nuh - don't

Nuff - plenty; too much

Numba - number

Nyam - to eat

O

Odda - other

Ole - old

One guinea - twenty-one

shillings - British currency

Oonuh - you all

Outa - out of; out at

Ova - over

P

Pan - on; pond; baking tin

Pee pee - urinate

Pickney - child

Pilla - pillow

Pint - point

Poas/Pos - post; to mail

Potata - potato

Powa - power

Preke - poppy-show; clown

Q

Quat –dung - sit down or stoop

Quata - quarter

Quiat - quiet

R

Raise-cane - outrageous behavior; quarrel

Renk - rude or feisty; foul; smelling bad

Renkin - rude

Res - rest

Rida - rider

Righted – in a good frame of mind; correct and with sense

Roun - round

S

Sah - sir

Salid – solid

Salid pint – solid point

Secon - second

Seh - say; said

Shet - shut

Shudda - should have

Siah - listen or look here

Sidung - sit down

Sista - sister

Sinting - something; a thing that you don't feel like calling the proper name.

Skillengton - skeleton

Slippas - slippers

Soma - some of them

Soun - sound

Sumady - somebody

Stan up - stand-up

Strent - strength

Stronga - stronger

Suppa - supper

Swalla - swallow

T

Tank - thank; storage container for water

Tan - stand; stay; wait and see

Tan tudy - keep still or shut up

Tap - stop

Teacha - teacher

Tek - take

Tiad - tired

Tief - thief; to steal

Tink - think; foul smelling

Togeda - together

Tree - tree; also the number three

Trough - through

Trow - throw

Tun - turn

U

Unda - under

Uppa - upper

V

Vice - voice

W

Wah - what

Waise - waist or waste

Wanda - wonder

Wandas - wonders

Wasa - was

Wata - water

Weda - Whether

Weh - away; where

Whola - whole

Wi - we

Widout - without

Wirl - world

Wit - with

Woulda - would have

X

X-cep - except

Y

Ya, yah - you; here; also can mean yes

Yaad - yard, place of
residence; house; home

Yah so - over here; right here

Yuh - you

Yuh a - you are

Yuh ha - you have

Z

Zian - Zion

Zinc - sheet of metal

Zion -   this is the holy land
talked about by the
Rastafarians, which is
in Ethiopia

Phrases *defined*

Breeze pass — To pass by quickly.

Drop a sleep — To fall asleep.

Gimi a drop — Give me a ride.

Let de pus outa de bag — To tell a secret.

Me an' yuh ano size — We are not in the same age group.

De horse gone trough de gate aready —

>The horse has gone through the gate already.

>Whatever happened has happened already, you cannot stop it.

Mek no sense cry ova spill milk —

>Makes no sense crying over spilled milk.

>Makes no sense worrying over what has already happened.

Nuh bada go tell Tom, Dick an' Harry —

>Do not go and tell other people.

Trouble nuh set like rain —

>Trouble don't set like rain.

>Rain gives warning because the sky gives warning by its dark clouds, but trouble comes when you do not expect it or without warning.

In de fambly way —
    Person is pregnant.

Unda de quiat —
    In secret.

Mi nuh trus' nuh shadow afta dark —
    I do not trust any shadow after it gets dark.
    I do not trust any one I do not know.

Bread butta pan two sides —
    Having everything to one's convenience.

www.ingramcontent.com/pod-product-compliance
Lightning Source LLC
Chambersburg PA
CBHW032013240626
47153CB00003B/1239